The Bones of It

First published in 2015 by
Liberties Press
140 Terenure Road North | Terenure | Dublin 6W
T: +353 (1) 405 5701 | W: libertiespress.com | E: info@libertiespress.com

Trade enquiries to Gill & Macmillan Distribution
Hume Avenue | Park West | Dublin 12
T: +353 (1) 500 9534 | F: +353 (1) 500 9595 | E: sales@gillmacmillan.ie

Distributed in the United Kingdom by
Turnaround Publisher Services
Unit 3 | Olympia Trading Estate | Coburg Road | London N22 6TZ
T: +44 (0) 20 8829 3000 | E: orders@turnaround-uk.com

Distributed in the United States by
Casemate-IPM | 22841 Quicksilver Dr | Dulles, VA 20166
T: +1 (703) 661-1586 | F: +1 (703) 661-1547 | E: ipmmail@presswarehouse.com

ISBN: 978-1-910742-02-0
2 4 6 8 10 9 7 5 3 1

A CIP record for this title is available from the British Library.

Cover design by Karen Vaughan – Liberties Press
Internal design by Liberties Press

The publishers gratefully acknowledge the financial assistance
of the Arts Council of Northern Ireland.

*All characters in this book are fictitious, and any resemblance to
actual persons, living or dead, is purely coincidental.*

The Bones of It

Kelly Creighton

LIB
ERT
I ES
NORTH

A child's life is like a piece of paper on
which every passer-by leaves a mark.
—Chinese proverb

12 March

Of course I know what you're really after.

All you really care about is Klaudia. You don't want to hear about me at all. It's always her – always Klaudia – people are on about. People get themselves all hung up over her, up and above everything else.

I know what it is: it's that photo of her at the lighthouse. For months it was her Facebook profile picture. It makes people think they know her, they've seen it that often. For ages it was all over the papers, all over the Internet. It was like she'd turned into a celebrity when it first happened. You see, she had this girl-next-door appeal about her. Nothing threatening. She was much more subtle than that. For a good while even I was duped.

Naturally Klaudia was far from being that person they've all painted her as. People don't know her at all. Of course they don't. You wouldn't be asking all these questions if they did, wouldn't be asking me to write about what happened to her, even though you sandwich your questions in between other ones so I won't get offended. So that I'll speak.

Anyway, if I'd known Klaudia at all, I'd have known to stay well clear. It's too late to change these things now at any rate.

Thinking about what happened prior to October – 'prior to October', you've coined that term – makes me think that maybe you have a point with this writing malarkey, this writing for therapy. Is that what you'd call it if you were speaking to anyone else but me?

I'm starting to think it couldn't hurt. Giving it a crack. Sure, you're always saying that even if I don't feel like telling you outright, even if it's just for myself and I choose to never show you, it would be good for me, would give me answers. There's always this search for them, isn't there? Why this? Why the fuck that?

But it's certainly not like Klaudia was the only thing that ever happened in my life, despite all this fascination with her.

The thing *is* that Klaudia *is not* the thing, and if I tell you about her then I have to tell you about Perry's Nurseries. And if I tell you how I came to be working in Perry's then I'll have to tell you about why I had to leave Newcastle in the first place. Of course, I can't tell you about that, about my homecoming, without mentioning Granny and her feeding tube, not without mentioning my da.

I'm not wasting my time on him.

These things all come as a package. People say bad things happen in threes. Wouldn't you? I would.

Funny how this time last year I hadn't even met Klaudia, yet now we'll always be linked. I'll not call it fate. The day we met, I was sitting outside, as was usual in Perry's, potting pansies, when Klaudia called over to me from a couple of rows away, asking if I needed some help.

Well, even though I said I was fine, she came over anyway, knelt beside me, honey-toned arms sallow against the bottle green of her work polo shirt. She was smiling to herself, a smug kind of a smile like there was some secret she was itching to tell me. Klaudia introduced herself in that smoked Polish voice of hers.

'Klaudia with a "K".' She offered me her hand to shake.

'I'm Scott,' I reciprocated.

But you know what? She was better in the flesh, her smile-raised cheeks almost hiding the cornflower blue in her eyes. You'd have missed that in her black-and-white photo at the lighthouse. Her eyes were bright and sparkling, and her skin was untranslatable in all mediums, except in person.

Klaudia's hair was darker at the top, dark to her cheekbones then blonde for the remainder: 'ombré', that hair colour's called. Two-toned. I saw it in a chick-mag once or twice back in Newcastle, loads of the uni girls wore their hair like that too. Hair breezing around her face, Klaudia took a band from her wrist and tied it back, the shorter layers at the front framing her jaw, arms raised so I could see the stubble-shadow in the crease of one armpit.

I swept the stray soil from the brim with my hand brush, back into the pot wedged between my knees. When she arranged her gloves onto her hands I noticed how tiny her wrists were. They reminded me of the games the kids in my primary school would've played, you know, those universal rules? Making you prove that your middle finger would snugly meet your thumb when wrapped around the opposite wrist? They should've been the perfect fit or there was something wrong with you. Or getting you to sit on the playground floor, and winch one of your shoeless feet up so you could measure it against the stretch of your own arm, between elbow and wrist.

Telling you it should be the exact same size or you were a freak. Telling you that your feet were small, and that small feet meant you must have small meat.

Klaudia looked at me like she was sizing me up: a tailored, cutting, kind of smile.

'Daniel Day Lewis or Johnny Depp?' she asked.

'What's that?' I was frowning, thinking I'd misheard her. Her accent was quite thick until you were used to it.

'Who would you rather? Daniel Day-Lewis or Johnny Depp?' Then a little chuckle.

'For what?' I was uncomfortable under her gaze.

She shrugged.

'I don't mean for deep philosophical conversation,' she said.

I looked at her line-free face and decided she was about twenty-five, which would've made her four years my senior. I was wrong.

'Oh, I don't know.' I skimmed her with my eyes. 'They're both good actors, I s'pose.'

'Not for acting.' Klaudia's eyes had a glint in them, and her cheeks pinked. Something in it made my palms sweat.

'Sure, Depp and Day-Lewis are both old boys now.'

'So?' asked Klaudia.

'*So?*' I parroted. 'Well, who would *you* rather then?'

'Daniel Day-Lewis. Every time. I like Irish men better than Americans,' Klaudia told me. 'Men here are very nice. Very brooding.'

'Aye, that's one word for them,' I said. She'd made me think of Da, how he'd have had to stop her there, would've shoe-horned in that, in Northern Ireland, you can't go around assuming that everyone identifies as Irish. I could picture him saying, 'Here, Klaudia, love, watch who you're calling Irish around here. Some of us are British, ya know!'

But what I'm talking about, about how Klaudia seemed to have something to say about everything, was a good thing, if a bit frothy. And although her chit-chat was air-filler, I couldn't see anything wrong with it.

In fact, every time we'd share a shift, Klaudia would tell me, in painstakingly minute detail, everything she'd done since we had last worked together. She'd ask me: 'What would you rather, be at home or be here?' Obviously there, at Perry's, with her. 'What would you rather, a garden full of pansies or a garden full of tulips?' I didn't care. Any garden would've been nice. Tulips, I'd have said.

She'd ask every mad sort of variation of the question, gardening-related or otherwise. It showed me that there must've be a kernel of light-heartedness in me still, if I was enjoying listening to her so much that I was starting to, at that stage, live for those shifts. Klaudia asked me which type of music I preferred. I was only allowed to choose dance music or disco. No alternatives. Yet I liked the alternative. I told her the Smashing Pumpkins were my favourite band.

'No, Scott! They are *too* before your time,' she said, like that meant a jot.

So I chose. I chose dance. When I was pushed into a corner, I could make a decision. It didn't have to be over thought. It was like I was coming out from behind a cold, dark rock.

But the funny thing about Klaudia was lunchtimes. (You'll want to know this, because she was already showing the transformation.) I'd orchestrate my breaks to coincide with hers. I'd drop myself into the seat opposite and ask Klaudia about herself. In the staff room, alone together, without ceramic pots to provide the acoustics between us, she'd go quiet. She'd be looking at the clock, just ignoring me.

'How long have you been living here? Not in town . . . NI, I mean,' I asked her. 'It must be a good long time, your English is excellent.'

She nodded.

When there were no distractions Klaudia was silent, as if she only functioned to outside sounds – background voices, scissor snips, the hissing of bees.

In that room there'd be no reply to anything, no matter what I asked. Klaudia chewed in tiny, thoughtful mouthfuls. She said nothing, only gave a pleading smile like she just wanted me out of her hair.

Klaudia had her mouth covered by one cupped hand, her cheeks – mid-chew – blushing so hard I was more prickled by her embarrassment than I was by her abrupt about-face in responsiveness. I lifted a tabloid from the scatter of them on the table and started to flick through the pages we'd soon frequent ourselves.

When she finished eating, Klaudia stood to leave.

'You've ages yet,' I usually reminded her.

'I don't mind,' was her usual response, as she slipped back to her duties early.

I didn't know if it was a cultural thing – I still can't tell – but Klaudia never spoke with her mouth full, like Granny used to tell me was the right way, and all those other elements in her code of conduct I've seemed to drop along the path.

The 'right way' has become irrelevant. Everything adults teach kids to be they've long forgotten themselves. Now we expect that you can, indeed, talk with your mouth full. Apparently you can do anything as long as it's only yourself you're hurting.

For Klaudia there was no point worrying about those little

things: conduct, propriety and so on, when she so callously disregarded the big things. That's what I'm telling you.

17 March

A year ago I was sitting in front of the dean of my – imminently ex – university. It was a foundering afternoon, winter didn't know it was supposed to have moved on already and the office was lit by the sad light of a desktop Tiffany lamp.

Da was fingering a tuft of stuffing that was poking out of the side of an old leather armchair that had been pre-positioned by the dean so that Da would be facing him, which Da had shuffled around so it was tilted more towards me, so I wouldn't miss the V-for-victory vein bulging at me from the centre of his furrowed forehead.

The dean said, 'Scott, there is no doubt that you're a bright young man, but I can't ignore what you've done, uncharacteristic or not.' He was sighing all over the place, pinching the top of his nose, his eyes almost closed like he was so bored that he was going to fall asleep any second. It was as though he kicked students out every day of the week.

In my two and a half years there I'd only ever heard of one other person being given the boot: a guy who'd smashed up the mirrors in the Students' Union toilets during Freshers' Week. He kicked the taps off the sinks too. We'd both signed on for the same course. First-year Politics. But then he never made it to any classes.

The only time I saw the guy was the night he caused all the damage. He was slumped over the sink boking his ring, probably from the pain in his toes, which he must've broken in the process, I'd imagine. The bouncers came and trailed him out of the place. Then he was gone.

Then there I was, thirty months after him, getting a taste of the dumb bugger's exit interview.

Some people just aren't cut out for university. I reasoned then that it was like caging a wild dog, like expecting to train wild ivy. Wild. Clue's in the name.

Da had a right gob on him, like he'd been expecting it all along. I was always going to disappoint him. Disappoint him that I wasn't like him, then disappoint him that maybe I *was* after all.

'Can you not just punish Scotty, like?' Da asked the dean.

Yes, 'Scotty'! A first time for everything. It was a day of firsts all right.

'The woman isn't pressing charges, and Scotty didn't *do* any damage to the car after all.'

The dean's face crumpled. I could see that he was thinking Da's a complete moron and, to be truthful, he is. When I started at uni he didn't know what higher education was, let alone that further education was anything after GCSEs, which he still called 'O levels', refusing to change anything about himself to meet the evolution of the rest of the world, even if that left Da standing, looking into a big bubbling abyss of dumb.

I sat there watching the two old sods act out their drama. I was itching to interrupt and say, 'Yes, dean. Give me a hundred lines. I shall not steal a car and joyride it through the streets of Newcastle upon Tyne again. I shall not steal a car and . . .' Well. You get the picture. Instead I just sat staring at a slice of wall that was pushing the wallpaper off itself. The room smelt like the bottom of a used flowerpot.

Da and me had sat there like that before, for my entrance interview. That was a funny thing. Not that I laughed then. In that first interview, in the School of Geography, Politics and Sociology, Da's face was a picture. He's self-righteous to the hilt, honest to God. He'd argue that Pete Doherty is a poet and not a junkie – listen, Da couldn't tell you a Babyshambles song from the Babychams Granny used to drink at Christmas before the tube went in. In fact, he wouldn't know a Babyshambles song if it came up to him and said, 'All right, Duke McAuley, how's it hanging? I'm a Babyshambles song, ya know?'

Duke McAuley, my sweet old pa. As you're well aware.

The thing about Pete Doherty being a beautiful poet or some such guff, Da read it somewhere, Elton John or someone said it. I can't be positive who it was right now because I wasn't fully listening. I just let Da ramble on. (Top tip: that's the way to deal with him next time you cross paths.) But there have been a handful of times in my life when I've said: 'No, Da, you're going to listen to me for a change.' I don't think it did any good.

Anyway, you want to have seen Da's face when the dean spoke, that first time. Da was like a child, all nods, big grin, prodding me with a jaunty elbow, 'Oh aye, he's very political, is Scott,' he said, even though, with every wave under the Stena Line ferry on the way over, all I'd got out of him was, 'Why politics of all things?'

He didn't want me to become a politician. Da claimed he wanted me to become a plumber. It was his *dream* for me. Apparently. Sounded more like my worst nightmare. Pipes and plastic. Pish and shite. Always prattling on about the amount plumbers could charge for doing fuck-all-squared, he was.

When the shower was clogged up in Granny's house and you had to stand heel-deep in cold backwash, Da had to fork out a hundred quid for someone to come in, spend five minutes, and basically say that it was just bunged with hair, that if he'd clean the bloody thing it would work. Well, as you can imagine, Da cracked right up.

But that was a good career to him, being a plumber – you know, being able to fleece people because they don't have that wee nugget of knowledge that you have? That was the thing he would've liked me to have done. A plumbing course was all it would've taken to make him proud. Big Duke was easily pleased!

But how can you be sure that anything would've pleased him? Nothing would've made a difference. I know now it was all in vain.

Last March, in comparison – that second time in the dean's office – Da came across just as stupidly. He was *begging* the dean to keep me on, until the dean leant forward on the table, hands interlocked, and peered over his glasses at Da.

'Mr McAuley, I think that Scott would benefit from counselling,' the dean said.

The dean gave me a sideways glance. At least he had the decency to half-acknowledge that I was still in the room, listening to them rip the knickers out of the whole thing. The remark threw me, I'll admit. I mean, *counselling*?

Da had a sneer on his face. 'Come on, I mean he shouldn't have done what he did, but *counselling*? Wha'?'

Come on, say it Da, I thought. *Say that you're a counsellor and you'll make me your own personal project via text messages if they allow me to stay here.* But he didn't. Didn't bring it up at all, for once.

'There are other things. There are confidentiality matters, so I will not digress.' The dean looked straight at me, and his stare hardened. Or maybe it was just because it was me he was looking at, because I was feeling it, because I knew exactly what he was talking about. It was Jasmine.

For the first time, I lost my cool, although, don't get me

wrong, I wasn't exactly sitting there all cool as you like: I was wee *scaredy Scott*, taken to blinking and staring at his boots, until he mentioned the *other things*. I shuffled in my chair, and my clasped hands slipped off each other. The hard beat of my pulse pumped in my ears.

'What's all this about?' Da snarled.

I shot a look at him. I'd thought he was talking to me, the way he said it. He wasn't. Da was on the defensive, his venom aimed at the dean instead. Regardless of the shit I'd have to endure afterwards – which came as thick as it did fast – Duke McAuley's son was being talked badly about. It stood for something back then.

The dean had his palms up, determined not to go any further, as if he'd said something he shouldn't have, as if he regretted having moved away from joyriding, to Jas.

But of course I wouldn't mention her name, not in that smelly room with its decomposing walls and chairs. *I'd* hauled myself over into the driver seat that night with Jasmine. I was happy to take the rap. Well, not *happy*, but you know what I mean.

And there *were* other things: Jasmine's da was a bastard too. I knew he'd contacted the uni. Look, I was out on my arse no matter what I said, why even bother trying to hold on?

Da got on his high horse.

'Tell me what you're on about. What can you not *digress*?' he was barking across the desk, sixty-fegs-a-day man that he is.

I withered further in my seat, like I'd been sprayed with weed killer and left in the sun. *Keep away from children and pets.*

'Stealing a car is sufficient, I feel. If Scott has anything else he wishes to talk about . . . a *professional* might be the way to go.'

Da relished the opportunity to go off on one. The word was an insult to him.

'We're out of here, Scott,' he said.

Where was 'Scotty', then? He nearly sent the seat under him flying across the wooden floorboards. That was him out of the door, but not before jabbing a finger in the air and booming at the dean, 'Go and shove your wanking university education up your fucking arsehole.'

'Sorry,' I mumbled at the dean, more on account of my da than anything else. I told Da I needed a slash before we hit the road, and I went to the loos, and I took a black Sharpie from my bag and I wrote 'Big Duke sucks donkey cock' on the back of the door. Popped the lid on the pen and myself out of there, into the big wild wilderness of freedom, and the fear that comes with escaping the cage.

Big Duke himself met me outside. He was lighting one up.

'Joke, so they are,' he repeated over and over, lips smacking the filter into a little wedge, his eyes screwed up to avoid the smoke.

He sat in his car, yanked the overflowing ashtray out, set his cig precariously into the plastic piping and turned on me.

'Why didn't you tell your man there that your Da's a counsellor?'

I knew it was coming. He could've done it himself, but he hadn't. Da knows that some things stick to people, like their names. McAuley, Northern Irish, counsellor: the dean would put it all together. He'd remember the headlines and see what happened after them. A politics man after all, one of the few people in England who would have an interest.

The drive to the boat was quiet, stretch after quiet stretch. Some of my gear was packed up in the back, but we'd left most of it behind. I didn't deserve a van loaned from a mate this time, unlike when I'd gone over to England in the first place. The Ikea furniture he'd treated me to was all left for the next person in the student house. Kyle and Farris were most probably calling dibs on it before I was out the door. Flogged on Gumtree maybe. Who knows?

After we stopped at a service station to refuel the car and ourselves, Da threw me the keys. 'You driving?' His joke with a jag. A ring of truth around it. He knew I couldn't – never had a lesson, not even one. It was one of the things in that long list that pissed him off about me.

He couldn't picture me in the driver's seat any more than I could picture myself there. I didn't care. There was no fight in me to state my case, you know? I was like a boxer who had started off hungry for a win and then lost all desire. It didn't matter. Nothing did.

Da jumped in the car, I handed him his keys back and he revved the engine. He didn't know how to hide his anger at having to retrieve me. Da knew somewhere in that big square head of his that I'd never amount to anything. Of course I wouldn't. Me, with all my privileges? The opportunities I'd received as a bizarre consequence of all the nonsense that went down when I was still in nappies, or 'diapers', as I later called them.

'Politics, of all things,' he started. 'What could you possibly know about it?'

It wouldn't have mattered if I had changed the subject – excuse the pun – politics got him like a barb under his skin. He was damaged by something he called politics, used politics as an excuse to do damage.

'I know plenty about politics now I've nearly got a degree in it,' I said.

My voice, though weak as water, nearly never left me. You could say things to Da that would nark him, if you did it in a defeated way that he was happy enough with. A slightly different tactic from your Klaudia question-sandwiches, but the same all in all.

'Well, you've nothing now, Sonny Jim. May as well've not done it,' Da said.

I took my sandwich out of its triangular plastic box and bit off the corner.

'Cheese?' Da asked.

'Cheese.'

Yes, cheese annoyed my da. As long as he'd known me I was a vegetarian, but he always offered me meat. Even in the service station, he couldn't say: 'Do you want cheese and ham? Tuna?' Nothing like that. He was like: 'Meat feast, Scott?' Just OTT, you know? Anybody else could've lifted a cheese sandwich and he wouldn't have given them the earache for it. But me? It was a sign of being a pink-blooded male, knowing his thought process.

I never drank coffee either, just tea, and preferably green. Da would go: 'Coffee, Scott?' He'd do it for badness, and I'd go: 'Yes. Black. Three sugars.' It isn't me, just *so not* me that anyone just meeting me for the first time would laugh it off and say: 'That's right, you're a green-tea man, Scott, aren't you?' Even *you* know that, though green tea is a thing of the past now. But Da would just pour the thing, complete windup merchant that he is. I'd just let it go cold and get a faint spider-skin on the top.

'You've let that get cold now. Do you want it micro-dinged?' he'd go.

I'd go, 'Aye, Da. Go on.'

This all sounds petty, I know, and I'm sorry. This isn't what you want to hear. It makes out, too, like we were always eating and drinking together and we weren't. But it's like any seldom time I did see the man, he had to be putting something to his lips to have a reason not to talk: like his fegs, coffee cup or sandwiches. All some mad excuse not to speak to his own son. That's probably why, when I came home from university, and he moved into Granny's house with me, Da put on a couple of stone in weight, at least. And he was already a big hulking bastard.

I doubt he ever intended on breaking away from his prisoner bubble in the city. Men who'd stabbed people, men who'd beaten their partners, Da had plenty of time for those people – on the surface – but for his mother, for his son, nothing.

If you love him, my da has no time for you. So don't. Don't fall for it.

Little grated bits of cheese were falling on my jeans. He was glancing at them.

'Give me a laugh, tell me what you were going to do with the politics.' He said 'the politics' the way he says 'the Tesco's' or 'the Facebook'.

'You work in politics,' I said. We were in Scotland at that stage, I reckon.

'Aye, that's different, what d'you know about it, from *County Down*?' He gurgled the words.

I was only from County Down because of him, because of fate, because of Granny's move from Belfast to escape the shame of people knowing she was related to him. Only there because of her kindness, or duty, or love, or whatever it was that took me from that water-filled hall in our old terraced house in Belfast, after he was locked up and after Mum had gone.

And there was nobody else. What did he want? Me taken into care? Passed about like a parcel that nobody wanted? Hell, sometimes fate takes its time.

He would've hated me going into the system at the time,

would've been relieved that his mum – my granny – was at least prepared to be there for his son, if not for him. Not at that time.

But now that I'm a man, the thought of me, not as a defence-less abandoned toddler, but *middle-class me* – and *grit-and-graft Duke McAuley's* middle-class son, no less – was it more damaging in the long run? I mean, I was now a man. He had the time and the hindsight to look back and decide that a bit of hardship wouldn't have done me any harm.

Would it have knocked the poncey, veggie, green-tea-drink-ing shite out of me? Maybe it would've.

'Politics is broader than *the Troubles*,' I said, expecting a full-on slabbering match to erupt, which obviously I was in no posi-tion to win, considering.

He just shook his head like I had no idea. 'You reckon so?'

I put my foot on the dashboard to tie the lace of my green Doc Martens boot. I used to love those boots. Lived in them.

'Everything is politics,' I said. I thought about politics then. It was true, politics was everywhere. Forget the lecture halls, there was politics in my student house and all around Jasmine like a glass case. Politics got me kicked out and kept away from her.

You can't argue with politics. It is what it is.

We all are.

10 April

Perry's used me up while there was potting and pruning to be done, and then there wasn't the need for so many staff members and our supervisor, Hugo, scarcely had me on the rota for one evening shift per week.

One night I helped a tree surgeon out to his van with sup-plies he'd ordered in for a bulk discount. Clint, he was called, so named after his ma's fanny flutters for the cowboy types, I presumed. Like Mr Eastwood himself, Clint was quiet, though friendly enough. We got to talking, and I asked him if he'd any extra work on and if he'd consider bringing me along. I was looking to be occupied more than paid, if I'm honest. He said that jobs were very few and even further between. The usual war cry. That he'd give me a shout, if and when things picked up. Clint got me to write my mobile number on the back of one of his business cards. It was a while before I heard from him.

I spent my time in the house again, trying to keep out of Da's way in the evenings. It turned out that he was a nine-to-five man after all, even though when I was growing up he never seemed to be free any particular time. Granny would call him on the landline, relay his full schedule back to me as I sat doing my homework at the kitchen table. He couldn't take me out because he had meetings at night, prison visits in the day and weekend talks to give in community centres dotted around Belfast.

Da was all about himself and his 'fellas', as he called them, gathering all the wrongdoers in Belfast into a little cluster under one grimy wing. Da felt privileged and wanted to play at peacemaker.

Then, when we lived together in the town, I was in the know and knew his timetable. Da was about more than I thought he'd be, and with me not driving, and having very little cash in my pockets, we were forced together.

In the month of April, he'd been to three of his fellas' funerals by the tenth of the month already. The irony of the hat-trick wasn't lost on him. That was a year ago today.

There's no coincidence in that either, that's why I'm telling you this now.

Anniversaries stir up all sorts of emotions.

I hadn't known the deceased, I was like a spectator that day in the chapel. I picture my da standing at the front of the funeral, an image I can't get out of my head. I remember him saying that it was fifteen years exactly from the Good Friday Agreement. It was a Wednesday though. What a pity that didn't correlate just for him.

My da . . . now there's a real celebrity, unlike Klaudia. He earns a living from his stories. Least he did *prior to October*.

I don't know if he still feels as privileged. It makes me smile, a bit. But of course, not for what happened, just the thought of what it might have done to Da's ego.

He knew I had no shift that day of funeral *número tres*, so he dragged me along. I wore the suit I'd got for my uni interview and it stirred it all back up again for Da. His sore points pointed to me. I only had one tie to my name, a tie-dyed jobby. 'Your hippy tie,' Da called it, and he lent me a black one. Da had a rack full because he either loves that colour one helluva lot or he's practically a professional mourner, if he's a professional anything.

In the car Da said, 'To some, this country's bid for peace was a cynical ploy, back in the day.' He always said things like that, and probably still is if anyone wants to hear what he has to say anymore. That was Da's thing – his non-political politicalness.

He started on about my degree again. 'Do you not wish you hadn't wasted everybody's time?' he said between tuts, confused, as if he was trying to align the colours on a Rubik's Cube, which is actually pretty easy when you know how. All in the algorithm.

I wanted to say that he should've understood, but I knew what his usual piffle would be, that what he didn't understand wasn't worth understanding, and I didn't want to hear it, not again. Anyway, Da was neutral now: no win, no fee, if you like. Didn't identify either way.

He was the 'Other' box on a monitoring form.

'People change,' as Granny always said. I wonder about her too.

Granny's tube runs up her nose, and it flexes down into her gullet, irritating the skin around one nostril. She has to dress it with a baby-fingertip portion of Sudocrem to keep the skin from breaking out. When she swallows, the tube pushes against the walls of her throat and makes her feel as though she's about to cry. Granny's in a permanent state of upset – I can still see it – it can't have been helped by the things that happened six months ago and all began this time last year, or God only knows when . . . decades ago.

'Spare a thought for the poor fella whose funeral we're driving to,' Da said, as if I weren't. No idea what went on in my head. 'Conor was a casualty of politics.'

He got all thoughtful, chewed at the cuticle on his thumb. 'Nah. That fella didn't quietly overdose by himself, he threw himself off a fucking bridge on a busy Saturday night in the city,' Da said, as if I didn't read the papers or look at the *Bel Tel* website, or hear his updates about people who were strangers to me but who he talked about as if I should be bent double, crying my heart out for their troubles.

'I'm sick of these Sunday-morning calls, telling me another fella's taken his own life.'

He didn't look sick to me, he seemed to dine on the drama like it was a honking great steak, tobacco onions on the top. He was practising, I soon realised, getting ready for the main event, which was him, of course. The headliner.

When we got to the chapel, my da stood, introducing himself

as Conor's counsellor, telling people he wasn't surprised at how he'd went, because 'Callum always lived life without a net.' People were looking at him as though he was mental. Besides everything else, he'd used the wrong name. Callum was our next-door neighbour in the town. *It's easy to get them Catholic names mixed up, sure they're made up, random letters pulled out of a Scrabble bag and rearranged, like.*

Da neglected to introduce me. It was the Duke McAuley show, evidently.

Then I realised, his is a name some people will never forget in parts of Belfast, although he sneakily introduced himself as Edward, not Duke, and his formerly roaring ginger hair – he once stood out for a mile – had over the past decade toned down.

I realised I wasn't there to be shown how lucky I was, grown up by the sea in Granny's little pebble-dash two up two down. I was there, instead, for hand holding.

Conor's Mum was open jawed, glass eyed, doped up with meds to get her over the service. Da made a beeline for her, clinched his hands around one of hers and told her not to worry. As if it was that simple. Da wanted to say a few words about her *boy*, her thirty-five-year-old boy, and she was too fixed on numbing pills to say no. She gave a lolling, disjointed nod, which was all he needed to proceed.

Conor's Mum was simply going along with the day, Jesus knows she didn't know what to do, never buried her child before, but Da had it 'down pat'. My hand to God that's what he said!

'This's my third of these dreaded things this month,' Da told her, nearly boastfully. *Dreaded, yes, these suicides thingamabobs are DREADFUL, tut-tut.* Her eyes glided over Da. He was on to the next thing before she got the chance to respond.

The priest had one of my hands squeezed in between the two of his at that point. He was a young southerner with a baby face and a lovely warm brogue. He took my gaze from Conor's mum and my own da for a moment. When I caught a glimpse of the pair again – the priest had moved on to the next in line – I recognised something in the weight of Conor's mum's eyes. Familiarity. Maybe pain? Or was it possible that it was stone-cold relief? I believe so.

It wasn't the first time she'd lost her son, if you get me. She'd lost him to crime, probably to the white powder – they're all at it, but of course you'll know that and pretend that you don't – she'd lost him to prison, then finally altogether.

Going, going, gone.

She had that look every woman I've known has had, including Mum and Granny, mourning my da every time they'd to lose another bit of him, until they'd given up completely.

At the service the priest spoke first, gave a sermon which started off just great because of the soothing lilt of his voice, the ups and downs. He made everything sound at peace and lyrical, like he was reading from a Seamus Heaney poem or something. 'Mid-Term Break' maybe. I remember I liked that one. But his words, I didn't fully hear them.

He pointed out the fire escapes, the way people do, in case we spontaneously combusted into flames inside the chapel. If anyone would, Da would. There was the possibility of it.

'Many *peo*-ple ask me,' the priest said, flicking his sandy hair from his eyes, 'in sad, *som*-bre times like *to*-day, "How can you, *Fa*-ther, understand what it is *like* to lose a *chi*-ld, when you are *not* married, and will *nev*-er be a father yourself?"'

I was interested to hear the answer, but then he meandered around the middle, and I started to fidget with boredom. I was

feeling the lack of sleep catching me up, and a wash of restful-
ness coming in off the stillness of the congregation, like a breeze
from the seafront.

I think his question was rhetorical, like those articles you see
on Yahoo! 'How you can earn millions playing video games for
a living'. 'How you can tell if your other half is having an affair'.
They never give you a straight answer, just bullet points that
you could've identified yourself, no formula you can apply to
real life.

Anyway, this priest, he was called *Father*, and if you call
something a thing, it makes it a thing. Does it not? Wasn't he
everyone's father? Like God? God's minion? So maybe we all
knew the answer anyway. Maybe we never even required the
question.

I couldn't see my own father, then I could. There was the
back of his dome, shining like silver in the palm of Judas
Iscariot's hand. How had I missed that big head? He was front
row. Up at the business end.

The young priest finished and called Conor's brother Tony
to read a passage from the Bible, and then went and stood at the
side. I couldn't tell you which passage Tony read because it all
meant nothing to me. He was stumbling over the words and all
that jazz. You'd have easily known that he was as much a stranger
to Sunday school – or Mass, it would've been in their house, I
suppose – as I'd been to my version of religion all my life.

Tony had one of those shorn military hairstyles, greying tattoos skulking over the backs of his hands, a freshly inked one up
the left-hand side of his neck. Tony was one of the hardest looking guys I'd ever seen, to be perfectly honest with you. He closed
the Bible, wiped the back of his hand against his short, wet
nose, looked into the crowd at a midpoint somewhere near the

back. It felt like it was me Tony was looking straight at, but I knew I was just where his eyes naturally fell. Then came the flood. Full force. A deep, sobby cry.

Tony was choking on a story about when he and Conor were wee, and how they'd go to a rented house in Donegal every Easter with their mum and da. Conor and him had always shared a fusty room in this '*Father Ted*-type parochial house'. I shot a look at young Father Dougal then, pressed against the whitewashed wall, and thought, *They must hate that show, them priests*, but he was actually smiling as he had done before as he'd welcomed the mourners, only now it was without the undertones of remorse.

He was a trendy priest, Dougal. 'Down with the kids', as they say. That's a dodgy saying to put beside a priest when you think about it.

The laugh they'd have had, Tony recalled, even if they had inevitably fallen out from spending all day 'in each other's pockets', as he put it. The word 'inevitably' gave me comfort. Was it inevitable that Da and I would fall out too?

'Brothers, y'know?' Tony shrugged then, and blew out. There was a slight sigh of acknowledgement in the row behind me and a few nods of bowed heads in front. But I *didn't* know.

Tony told us how at night Conor would come alive and wouldn't shut up for anything, wanting to talk shite into the early hours, and their da would be shouting in at them to wise up, but they'd be giggling away, nothing stopping them.

'I'd be telling the stupid bugger to shut up too, but Conor was too infectious with that laugh,' Tony said inside a moment where he'd managed to catch his breath, stop fighting his emotion. Everybody seemed to recall Conor's laugh, which I could only imagine, of course, and never know if I'd imagined it rightly or imagined it wrongly. The thought of it gave a few mourners cause to echo it with their own stifled chuckles.

'Just a stupid wee story,' Tony said, 'the thing that keeps going round in my head.' He stirred the air beside his head with his index finger.

When he was done, before their da gave his short, tight speech, which has managed to slip through a crack in my memory, my da strode up to the front of the chapel. A lesson in calm and poise he was as he told everyone his findings, how he couldn't *not* look at statistics. He said, 'Despite everything, look, we're still tall and intact.'

But Conor was far from intact. He'd been scraped off the road like chewing gum lost its taste. His mum wasn't intact, she was falling apart in the front row, oblivious to her husband's arm around her. Only Da seemed intact, really, although I got the impression that Conor's da was a pretty steely old bastard too.

Da pressed his hands flat on the pulpit like it was a pizza base he was prepping for his toppings, and said, 'In our wee country the roads used to be the problem,' and then took a big dramatic pause you could've got swallowed up in and added, 'now it's the journey that's the problem. And you want to know something else?'

No, stop now. Please.

'There still isn't enough being done to support our prisoners, the ones who make it to the other side and don't finish everything from where they were, within those gates.' He pointed at the door as he said that. The priest stood squinting at him, with his head tilted in a way that was hard to read. 'And even if these fellas do make it out to the other end, they usually have their lives hindered by addiction.'

I'm not saying that Da didn't have a point – or two – and that I didn't care, in case that's how I'm coming across. I'm actually very sympathetic to the plight of prisoners, perhaps more now, I'd say . . . as I've gotten older. I can appreciate why returning to society would be hard, but I still believe that when you're crammed close to others you can make your own personal space. You can leave in your mind.

I had a tiny bit of compassion for Conor. I'll admit, it was hard not to after seeing the state of his mum. And, take Tony – it's not often I'd seen a man shed tears, especially not so openly. So sore. There's only one other time that really stands out.

Tony's face was a hand in my gut, wringing the weightiness out of my preconceptions of Da's fellas. What it means to be a man. No one had been made to itch by his public display of anguish, that was the thing. We were captivated, all of us congregated in the stalls who weren't even characters in Conor's story. It felt like a collective, heaving release.

I felt as close to tears as I'd allow myself. I really did. I'm not a machine, even though you probably think that I am. But it was Da's mention of addiction that jarred for me. That's where I neutered my sympathy.

Addiction isn't just a word or an abstract concept, not to the children of addicts. It's not a word to bandy about in churches and chapels, but a dull, achy reality.

I remembered our trips to the cinema. I remembered my da having vodka-tinged naps in the back row, and him blaring his horn, slabbering at the Sunday drivers who dallied along the back roads. He'd have been sheepish as he dropped me back to Granny's. He'd linger at the front of the house, asking me what kind of mood she was in, as if she had more than one. But she did, for her son. Granny had a whole array of emotions until she became like Conor's mum and decided to box off things that involved him.

She stopped expecting anything from Da – my 'alco-pop' – and she took on the listless expression she always wore in his presence. And that was just the times he showed up. Usually he was laying stocious somewhere and didn't bother his hole.

Then there were the times when Da did show, but he'd be half-cut, and Granny wouldn't trust him to drive me anywhere. She felt obliged to ply him with coffee first to sand the drink-edge off him before sending him on his way back to the city. Although she couldn't bear his drunken company, and neither could I. But kids can't say, can they?

We would tolerate him while he polished off three or four cups of Maxwell House, talked like an eejit, then wrestled the stairs to flood our toilet like a racehorse. We would stand smiling at each other in the kitchen at the sound of him pissing in the room above us, and Granny would explain to me that he was only still there until he sobered up because she'd never forgive herself if 'your da wiped some wee family off the face of the Earth with his motor.'

Why do people always take responsibility for other people's mistakes?

Why are we expected to?

In the chapel, no one realised that we were together. You'll understand we look nothing alike. Christ, we *are* nothing alike. Maybe in some deep-rooted way that there's no shaking off, but in person, in manner, in everything you can see and touch, there's nothing similar.

I'm five-foot-eight and 'fine-featured', as Klaudia called it. I'm the spit of my mum according to Granny. It's the dark hair mostly, though my eyes are brown and not the sea green Mum's were. I didn't know if resembling her was a good thing or not. I could never tell if Granny liked, pitied or loathed Mum. The dead stay as ghosts with Granny: confined to pictures, not talk, not like Da, the six-foot-two, larger-than-life Duke-boy, who I'm sure won't ever fade out, even when he does pop off. He'll always be talked about. Always bounce back like a swatted wasp.

Da's nearly spilling into his fifth decade, his hair now silver, exactly like Granny's. Da has ice-blue eyes that twinkle at the wrong times, like on that pulpit when he was saying, 'It's no coincidence all the men I've known to die these past ten days were all around the thirty-five years mark. Children of the Troubles. The recession's over but yet these people are still *so very* wounded. Why, when life should be getting better, is it not? And what is it about spring, the symbol for new life and regrowth? Up with this we will not put!' he shouts, certainly sounding political then, a throwback from his old paramilitary days.

The man beside me turned to his wife and whispered, 'Conor made his decision, his mother shouldn't have to sit listening to this.' He was the type my da would've said thought the peace process was a cynical ploy, if I'd have told him what he'd said. I should have. I was too bloody nice. A submissive saint is what I was.

The man's wife snickered. 'Poacher turned gamekeeper, your man here.'

After the show – I mean service – I went to the toilet and checked my phone. Klaudia had texted me. She always texted, didn't mind frittering them away. She got a hundred free a month. I thought they were all for me or why else would she have mentioned them?

'Food or water?' she was asking.

I smiled to myself. 'Water,' I texted back. I've known for a long time I could survive without food.

11 April

So ... the funeral. At the end of it Da introduced me to Conor's family, reclaiming me as his son. 'Scott's home from university for a few days.' He neglected to mention the part where I was never going back. *Sure, don't let the truth get in the way of a good story, Da. Will ya?*

'Studying politics,' Da said, his face brightening with something like pride. But not. That's impossible.

Conor's da shook my hand. 'Nice to meet you, Scott,' he said. He was dry, literally dry: dandruff had flecked onto his dark nylon shoulders in random constellations, skin granules flaked off his forehead and the sides of his nose. Dehydrated by death. He was like a snake shedding his old skin for this new one he had underneath, one more suited to the person he was going to be after that day. Not a widower and not an orphan. There's no name given to people who lose children, because it's too unthinkable. You told me that. Do you remember?

Then Conor's da turned to my da. 'It's a family burial only, *mate*.' The 'mate' was obligatory, it had a harsh 't' like a hard nut in the centre of something more palatable.

'Oh, of course. You're just right to invite family only, I would too.' Da gave his chin a scratch in agreement.

When exactly would he invite family only? Was he wondering about how he'd bury me? Had Da thought about the possibility that I'd go before him? Did my own father want me six feet under, and if it was family only that would mean just him and Granny – pretty sodding miserable – unless I got strangers dragged along to bulk out the congregation for me, too. A few stragglers who never knew me, pulled in off the street, maybe. It wouldn't be too much of a stretch to imagine him doing that sort of thing, you know.

'Do you want me to tell everybody the plan?' my da asked Conor's da. *The plan? The plan? Yes indeed. The three-step bury-your-son-with-ease plan. Money-back guarantee if you're not fully satisfied.*

'Everyone already knows,' he said, making sure the last one did, that da wouldn't latch on and be undislodgeable.

My phone vibrated in my pocket, I excused myself, went to sit in Da's car to take a look at it. Klaudia was texting again, taking leave from her hypotheticals, asking if I still wanted to meet later that evening. She needed to know if she should hurry back because she'd left for the market and ended up spending all day in the next town across, and if she wasn't meeting me then there was always some friend she would like to call in on. She was giving me first dibs, that was it.

I'd almost forgotten how, at 3 AM, I'd emailed Klaudia to ask if we could get together for a chat. I'd sat up late, watched a movie in my room and played Halo on my console. It was a gamer called PolesApart10 – who I was giving a good pummelling to, might I add – who first made me think of her, though Klaudia was never far from my mind. Still isn't.

She hadn't answered her phone when I called. Sometimes she switched to 'don't disturb' during the night, she'd already explained this to me so I'd stop taking it bad when she didn't pick up. Klaudia would get in touch when she could.

I'd taken my glasses off to rub the fuzziness of all those screen hours from my eyes. When I put them back on I caught a blurred glimpse of my reflection in the only photograph on my wall, a signed photo of Billy Corgan, the lead man from The Smashing Pumpkins.

It's the only photograph I bothered fixing to the wall of my bedroom, for a couple of reasons: for one, it seemed like the moment I let the hammer hit the wall – it only took two taps and it was done – that the doorbell went and Aoife from next door was on the doorstep in clothes Granny would call 'sloppy joes', her baby son in a white blanket encircled by her shaky arms. He had little sleepy seeds in his eyes and all. Red-eyed. Red-cheeked. Her too. Her mousey hair all over the place. She had none of Klaudia's girl-next-door appeal. Aoife was like a burst settee. I got the impression they'd both been gurning their lamps out well before I rolled my hammer back in the air.

She looked on the verge of throwing the child at me. For all I know I'd just saved the boy from a pillow over his face. Aoife asked me to have some consideration, added in that it was his bedtime. She caught me looking at Granny's grandfather clock darkly slumped in the hall, and pre-empted me saying that it was only lunch time, one o'clock or so, by saying that I wouldn't understand but that babies needed naps. *Scott's too thick to understand the obvious.* And if I was doing any 'banging' again could I let her know – *banging*, like! Two small taps. I was to ask her permission was what the woman really meant.

'Already done, just hanging a photo of Billy Corgan,' I said, thinking she was probably the right age, that she'd remember The Smashing Pumpkins. Klaudia would say the Pumpkins were more Aoife's time than mine, she'd allow *her* to like them in a two-option scenario.

I thought the mention of Corgan would remind Aoife of some happy memory before her life became a haze of postnatal whatever and all that shite. Maybe she'd lighten up, crack a fucking smile or something, but Aoife had no interest in me, and if she knew who I was talking about she didn't let it show.

I've found that everyone knows more than they ever let on.

She was like people generally are once they've had kids – that particular baby was her third, the world had been spinning just for her for a long time already by that point. Anybody else trying to inhabit her world – or even trying to live quietly at the other side of *her* wall – was nothing but an inconvenience to Aoife.

I didn't understand why people like her didn't just buy houses a bit out in the country, where there were no neighbours. I couldn't get my head around why she told herself she'd ever enjoy living beside other people.

Aoife went on about it, 'It's great round our way, it's quiet but there're plenty of wee ones to play with . . . once the boys get of an age.' That's the kind of tripe I've heard her say on autopilot, even when people are just saying hello to her and not wanting to hear her appraisal of our street. It was the postman once, then old Mrs Dudley, my primary-school dinner lady.

I remember once Dudley was walking her dog past our slice of the street. She had this bouncy walk, left hand swinging perpendicular to her hip. I suspect she still does. I was watching as she winked her dry acknowledgement of Aoife, as Aoife herself grappled her kids into their car seats, and I stood unlocking my front door, invisible as ever.

Aoife started a random conversation with Mrs Dudley. Never once asked Dudley anything about herself. Aoife thinks people without kids have nothing to offer a conversation. Actually, she didn't want a conversation, she wanted a listener. Well, her kids didn't listen to her, from the amount of shouting you'd hear.

She was shoehorning in how much she liked living there, blatantly bullshitting because the house had been intermittently on the market and going nowhere. Overpriced and under-cared-for. Occasionally she and Callum would lose the head, decide that while the street wasn't good enough for them, their home had the potential to be. They'd start half-arsed projects, paint the outside of the house without accounting for the top of it being six feet higher than their ladder, leaving a stripe of grey stone above the lemon masonry paint. Too cheap to pay someone to finish the rest or to buy longer ladders.

Then there were the prearranged wooden planters that went out of season and were never maintained. The deadhead plumage made me wonder how they could get three boys to the end of the day without them shrivelling up and rotting.

Maybe Aoife's monologues weren't for Mrs Dudley's sake anyway, nor the postman's, nor mine, although sometimes it felt like Aoife was saying things for my benefit. She was really giving herself the hard sell, trying to convince herself that she really did like living there.

It was bullshit. Her eldest boy was plenty old enough and she didn't let him go anywhere, and when kids called for him in their school uniforms that filled me with memories (and not good ones), she never let any of them over her door. I think she's a snob. I think the kids round our way didn't live up to the aspiration she had for her herself and her kids. Aoife would've preferred the neighbours from the development up the road, the nicely spaced-out bungalows, kids' bikes that straddled freshly mown lawns, full-of-life plants around the edges. She'd have loved that, Aoife.

At least she didn't live on 'the ranch', which is an estate tucked in our town's armpit. If she lived there, Aoife would've had something to complain about. There'd have been no complaining about tapping a wall or she'd have been put in her place. Neighbours on the ranch certainly wouldn't have been as peaceable as I was.

★

Aoife's baby gave me a tired smile and blew a raspberry against a wet, clotted fist. I reached out, gave him a little pat on the back like you would a dog's head. Not that I'd ever patted a dog before. I'd seen people do it on TV. I started to think about babies and about what being a father would entail. I liked to think that I wouldn't turn so crabbit, that I'd be a good dad. Patting the little mite on the head broke Aoife's sternness a bit.

'Okay, Scott' she said smiling, thin and schoolteacherly.

So that was Aoife, and partly why I just left it at the one picture. I had old movie posters that had been pulled down, the Blu-Tack had stolen little coins of paint from the woodchip along with it, but I didn't bother sticking anything else over.

Repainting anything was out of the question. Taking pride in our surroundings moved out along with Granny, so I suppose I have a bit of a cheek slagging Callum and Aoife. But they liked to think they were better than me, I think that's what I'm getting at. But really they weren't. That's all I'm trying to say.

I don't really *do* photographs anyway – except for the ones on my phone of Jasmine, and they're hardly what anyone would consider to be frameable – but I found a space for Corgan.

Listen, despite the certificate of authenticity I know it's a fake autograph. It's a good copy. You could rightly believe it's his handwriting. A fiver on eBay, more of a flimsy photocopy than a glossy, but still I liked it. God knows where it is now.

Corgan gets me. I could always tell he would if we were to ever meet because his lyrics spoke like they'd come straight out of my brain.

On the glass of the frame my sorry profile overlapped his, my short-back-and-sides head over Corgan's shaved one. I noticed my glasses sat half an inch above my ear. Klaudia had laughed about their positioning once. It was in Perry's. We'd spent all morning arranging a late-spring display. We'd taken a few steps back to assess the damage: the two vintage bicycles with amethyst flowers spilling out of their front baskets, the wicker planters with stiff lavender shoots scratching the bicycles' reedy spokes, the lilac bunting swooping down, flapping over the whole lot. It was at that point Klaudia asked, 'Do you wear children's spectacles, Scott?'

Of course I'd said, 'No. Why would you say that?'

She'd overdone it on the lavender, used too much purple instead of just accents of the colour like Hugo had told us Mr Perry liked to see, though Mr Perry himself never saw a thing. At least, I never saw him. His name was purely wheeled out when someone – namely, a supervisor with insufficient authority, in other words, old Hugo – wanted to close a case.

Klaudia ignored any tinny threats from Mr Perry. She had a vision of how she wanted the display to look and so she'd swept everything that was purple from every corner of the Nurseries, upending the settled displays for the sake of going to town on this new one.

Perry had bigger fish to fry anyway, in his massive home on the North Coast. He had a much superior version of the Nurseries right on his doorstep. It was the lunchroom talk. They all had the little brother complex about Perry, especially the part-timers, the mid-thirties working mums. The children of the Troubles, as Da would call them. Although only males were really affected, going by his stats. But you know not one of those frumpy cunts respected Perry for giving them a job in the first place.

'They are never where they should be,' Klaudia said.

She pressed the legs of my glasses down so they were snug at the sides, hooked tightly behind my ears. I felt the tips of her fingers on my temples. I was standing, looking at Klaudia, the Perry's Nurseries sign in the background. But it was all double-exposed.

My mum was there. I was wee – when I was wee was the only time I had with my mum – and she was sitting on the sofa in our gloomy Belfast house, her legs curled under her and me curled in her lap. The fragrant air – the lavender – cushioned my head like the softness of her chest. Mum circled her fingertips over my temples until I fell asleep.

Then Klaudia looked away and smiled like she was pleased with the display. That was the first sign that she wasn't connected to me. For one, she couldn't tell that something so big had dropped inside me with the graze of her fingers. *She* did it and she even didn't know. I couldn't tell if it was magic or a curse.

Do you know that I found it hard to get to sleep at Granny's at first, after Mum? I had restless-head syndrome. Apart from anything else the smells were different. There was no lavender spray, and I was expected to fall asleep on my own – Da had when he was young, he'd had a room on his own. Aren't all children the same? I didn't know how to ask for Mum's special temple rub. It isn't a fabricated memory of my mum because there was no one to ask, no one who could answer anyway. I know it's real.

Looking at Klaudia I saw Mum again, her eyes, the drift of them, calmly shooing me asleep, her arms rocking me. It was the first time I'd thought about Mum in years, *really* thought about her like she used to be an actual living person and not a dream. It started something, it grew until I felt like I needed to find out more about her.

★

Sitting in Da's car outside Conor's funeral, I looked at Klaudia's new text. 'I can see my friend another time. We can still meet up. Has something happened?'

I replied, 'What would you rather, a funeral or a wedding?'

The text was away before I could stop it. For crying out loud, she already thought I was interested, I could tell. I'm not overly experienced with girls, but even I could tell that Klaudia had notions about me. At times I saw her flinch.

When I'd told her about Jasmine she'd just told me about her ex. Klaudia had moved to the town with him a year before. He'd let her down, dumped her and left her with a mortgage and a fat ginger cat who was like a daughter to them both, she'd told me one night at the lighthouse with tears in her cornflower eyes. Marmolada she called it, sneaky little cretin. Cats don't help my asthma. I've always been a bit indifferent to their existence.

Klaudia once told me that the cat had taken over her bed, and she'd ended up sleeping on the sofa. That's the kind of thing that annoyed me. It made Klaudia sound like a real soft touch.

This wedding/funeral text was sent. Then no reply. 'It's just that actually I'm at a funeral,' I texted to clarify.

I watched my da linger, watched him shake the hands of everyone leaving, ingratiating himself with the mourners until every car was filled and navigated away.

'Hope u r ok :-(,' Klaudia texted me back.

I would be, when I saw her, I thought.

I slid the phone into my pocket. It buzzed again, Da slid into the car just as the phone rang. He tore strips off me.

'Scott. D'you not have that thing turned off?'

'Just switched it from silent this second,' I said.

'Oh, righto.'

He was a bundle of nerves, the façade slipping fast. He slammed the door shut and ran his hand over his face, propped his elbow on his window ledge and his cheek on the wedge of the back of his hand. My phone kept going.

'I'll just get this,' I said, like I was asking his permission. I hated myself for it.

'Go on then,' he was irate. Back to himself.

I took the phone back out of my inside pocket. It was Klaudia. Sure it was always Klaudia.

'Scott? Is . . . everything okay?' She sounded stop-start.

'Hi, yep fine.'

'But the funeral . . . ?

'Yes, umm, the funeral . . . I came along, that's right.'

Da was pausing around starting the engine, eyes on the *rosy apple*, ears on my conversation with Klaudia.

'Who has died, Scott?'

'Someone my dad worked with,' I said. 'A colleague of his.'

He glanced sideways at this. Looking back, I think I said that because she was my colleague, to show her that I was decent enough to do things like that. Conor wasn't even *my* colleague, I was such a *thoughtful guy*.

'I thought maybe something had happened to your grandmother with you phoning so late, or so early in the morning, in fact,' she said. Klaudia asked if the person was young.

'Thirty-five,' Da interjected pulling his mouth into a line, giving a head shake for good measure.

'Thirty-five,' I said.

'My goodness! Did he have any family?'

'No kids, thank God,' Da said, he could hear the whole bloody thing. Lapping it up, so he was.

'No. No kids,' I said.

Klaudia stayed quiet for a while, not often she was short for words.

'How did he die, Scott?' she asked. I liked my name in her mouth.

'Erm.' I pressed the phone to my ear with my shoulder as if it would absorb the sound. 'Did you hear about the guy in Belfast, fell from the bridge on the motorway?'

'Fell?' Da hooted. Owl of little wisdom.

'Threw himself, I mean,' I corrected myself.

'Oh my God, Scott, that is terrible. Listen to me, I will be back in the town at seven. Do you want to meet up?'

Da shot me a look, I pretended I couldn't see him, that all I could see was the blackness leaving, the colourful pedestrians jockeying up the road. The day returning to life.

'We're leaving Belfast now. Eight o'clock, okay?' I asked, buying time.

'The lighthouse?' Klaudia asked.

And that was that, we'd arranged where we'd meet and he'd heard the whole bloody thing. It grated on me and I couldn't tell you why then. The little things I hadn't pinpointed then.

I rang off the call. Da had this crazed grin on him.

'Klaudia, you call her,' I said. There I was again, explaining myself to *him*, as if I wasn't allowed a friend and yet I didn't have a clue where he went, when he did go out, and which *lucky* girl was the reason that his huge box of Durex Gossamers in his bedroom drawer was dwindling. Because he certainly never got the chance to use them when I was about. But whatever and whoever he was doing, I didn't care. What I did find amusing was how much he cared about all of my goings on.

'Klaudia?' he frowned.

'With a "K".' *Why? Why?* 'She's originally from Poland.' *And why again.*

'Flippin heck they're rightly getting about. Belfast was hiving with Eastern Europeans, which I can sort of understand . . . but the town? Christ Jesus, what's drawing them there?'

'Why not the town? It's a beautiful place to live.'

He gave a bluster, blowing outwards. Whinnying horse. When I used to see him – years ago, when he was still on the drink – it was *taig* this, *taig* that. Then – when he'd dried out – there were all sorts for him to dislike and not just the other team, the green team. Our wee country had turned into a nucleus, splitting and splitting, making new little pockets of people he was afraid to get to understand. But I think you can avoid fear by facing it.

Da changed from 'them', switched to 'the others', forgetting that he was a tick in the 'other' box, too. But he wasn't categorising. No, no.

'Sure, come one, come all. We're all individual.' Da didn't want to be made a hypocrite. Still had his peace-hat on. 'Hand us a Marathon bar out of the glove compartment,' he said, 'fooking starving here. Thought there might've been a sarnie on offer, at least.'

But I wonder how individual we are. I consider this sometimes, in bed at night, looking at the ceiling, feeling like it's nearly on top of me. I wonder if all women are as broken as Conor's mum, and if all men are as angry as Da, or maybe we're all just broken and angry, every single one of us. I know you wouldn't agree. You're paid not to.

'Where'd you meet *this* Klaudia?' It was accusing.

'Work,' I said, checking I'd rung off properly, that she wasn't listening to him down the line.

'Your age?' he asked, mouth full of Snickers. Da looked

delighted. Poor Conor, that distant inconvenient memory of him. Some things are more important. For instance, Scott might be getting his hole.

'A bit older,' I said.

'Older women can teach you a few things,' Da said.

'That right?'

'Don't get touchy. I'm only having you on, fuck sake.'

'She's a friend.'

'It's good you have one.' The sarcasm was dripping off him.

Da hadn't been around to know any of my friends. Saw more of the dean than he did of any teacher of mine over the years. That job befell Granny, it turned out. Da came into the picture too late.

It was frosty as hell in the car after our words. His words. Believe me, those twenty miles from Belfast to town felt twice as long. I was distracted by dust motes dancing in the light. Because I don't drive I see the glass. I've always wondered how it doesn't distract the driver. I'd watch the bubbles of rain playing dot to dot on the windscreen. We drifted along the road, on the Sydenham Bypass, past George Best Airport, bumping along on the patchwork road.

Once, ages ago, Da had an Elton John CD full of love songs – pah! He played it to death until he got dumped. My da doesn't like music – except that one brief brush with Elton. I mean, how can you trust a person who doesn't like music? Only a sad, pathetic bastard doesn't like music. Every car journey was a silent chore. Now, I'm no muso, I like classical and of course I'll always love the Pumpkins, but that would never wash with him.

When Da hears The Smashing Pumpkins, he always sings 'What's the Frequency, Kenneth?' by R.E.M., over the top, as if it's all the same to him. Good music, I mean.

When I got in the door I went straight to my room. I felt like

I had to meditate or else I'd burst. But I couldn't do it, my blood was boiling and, shoes off, on the floor, I kept closing my eyes only to see his face behind my eyelids: the scenes of us both since I'd come home from Newcastle.

I couldn't listen to *Mellon Collie and the Infinite Sadness*, it would've made me feel justified in my anger. I was justified, but I was looking for a distraction from it, because sometimes it's better that way, better to get it away from you. And so, I tried to turn on the radio instead for a poppy beat. An uplift.

I lay on my bed and listened to some tunes. No joy, I was still angry, my decent music was still in Newcastle along with my iPod, which would be in Kyle's pocket. Not that he liked that kind of music, but living in places like that is good practice for anywhere else you have to go where you need to live with people you would never choose to.

People get institutionalised pretty quickly. They shovel their dinner into them as if someone's going to take it away, they hold onto batteries like they're gold dust. It's what happens when you live in places full of people you can't trust. Little things become big things. And families are no better.

We all have our limits, even me, meek as I may come across at first. Little things seem big to me when there are enough of them piled on top of one other and I'm pushing to get out from under. Take now, for instance. The other day I was sitting outside, a fella was looking at me the wrong way. Not that there's a right way to look at someone, but he wasn't just blank, you know? I just want blankness from people who don't know me. Like how you were at first. You've studied the rule book, but this guy got it in his head he had to say something to me. I saw it coming. Let me tell you, life toughens you up or it breaks you. If my da had seen the way I handled this dickhead, he would've wondered where poncey Scott had gone. He might have wondered if he was right about me, if I do have problems.

The guy was walking over, eyes on the prize, when I started to scream, 'Come on then, what the fuck do you want?'

'Take it easy, mate,' he said. He sounded like my da. He was a lying toerag, this old boy. He'd been coming to me with intention. I know it.

'Copycat,' he snickered afterwards.

I have to watch out now for him, 'cause, like my da, he can't let sleeping dogs lie, this guy. They all have that same look in their eyes, clenched jaws. All that.

They think I'm quiet. But when I have something to say they will all hear me. I'm quiet because I'm so loud sometimes I'm all I can hear.

★

My answerphone caught her call too soon. I grabbed the suit crumpled over the chair in the corner of the room and I got my phone – Klaudia. I'd forgotten all about her. It was after eight. She'd left a voicemail: 'Hi, babe I'm here waiting for you, hurry.'

I pulled a checked shirt and jeans on, stepped inside my DMs, tucked the laces down the sides, and ran down the stairs, out onto the street, five minutes through town, to the lighthouse. When I got there she was about to get into her car.

'Klaudia, stop, please,' I managed to say, my lungs killing me. I excused myself before I turned my back and spat into a tissue I pulled from my pocket. The tissue was covered in blood from a scab I'd knocked the top off and had to stem back in my room. I kept the tissue in two cupped hands so she wouldn't see and ask why I hadn't just thrown it away.

It wasn't always easy to get rid of things like that. The council hadn't put a single bin in the vicinity of the lighthouse. Not one. The town was getting worse. The bank had closed down, there was only one functioning ATM. They were digging up the footpaths and taking their time finishing the job. Half the time we were walking over boards to avoid falling in a hole.

Klaudia had to find me a carrier bag from her handbag. Then we stood there, me holding a bag with a tissue in it with my phlegm and blood.

'What kept you so long?'

'The funeral. We had to go to bury the guy after. Couldn't get away from his mum, she was so upset.'

Klaudia put her hand to her chest, clutching a woolly heart in the material of her oversized cream jumper.

'Scott, that's awful. I can't believe he threw himself. Why did he do it?'

I had no idea what to tell her, I couldn't say that my da had murdered two men in the early 1990s, stabbed them to death after chasing and cornering them in an alleyway. I couldn't tell her that he had no reason other than they were Catholics, younger than him too, and a helluva lot smaller. I couldn't tell her that he only did five years because he was released under the Good Friday Agreement. What if she got scared by it? But maybe I should've said something. Maybe she needed to be scared. Scared off.

God knows Klaudia wouldn't have come here twenty years ago, but now the place was apparently so different. Da said there were casualties, people were still suffering. Me? I was surely okay, born just before change. Too young to feel the ripples.

'Who knows why people do these things,' I said to Klaudia, she walked toward the lighthouse, me behind her.

She turned back and smiled.

'Let's lift a shadow off the evening,' she said.

I was fine with that, I told her. She looked back at me. White silence. Klaudia joined me on top of the wall. The water was going against itself, the seagulls echoing each other. We played the what-would-you-rather game. It felt unnatural because she was clearly pissed off and so was I, but once we sat our arses on the stone wall and looked out across to the serrations of the island, everything slotted back into place.

'Sailing or flying?' Klaudia asked, her black patent brogues squeaking off each other when she crossed her ankles.

'I grew up here by the sea, so sailing, has to be,' I said. 'You?'

'Yes, me too.'

'How was the market?'

'Really good,' she said.

She took a mask out of her bag, a harlequin-type thing with black-and-white squares on it and a gold frilly edge. For a moment, Klaudia held it over her face.

'It reminds me of your profile picture,' I told her.

She frowned, a little wrinkle appearing between her brows, a worm of worry wriggling. 'I'm not wearing a mask. That is my normal face, Scott.'

'I know that, silly! It's the monochrome.'

'Oh. I collect masks, you know.'

She stroked the chin of it like an old man would stroke his beard, only more delicate. Tender. Her nails were bare. The nails of someone who worked in a nursery: short and practical, lengths slightly varied.

I reached out for the mask, held it over my face hoping that she would fix it for me. Touch me again. She didn't. Klaudia looked away, clasped her hands together, uncrossed her legs and rested her forearms on her navy-blue-and-white patterned leggings. She looked out at the water. 'When I was a little girl in Poland I used to make my own masks. I would smear petroleum jelly all over my brothers' faces and then get strips of plaster of Paris and stick them to their skin.' I imagined I could feel her hands as she talked, on my face, my skin tingling like it was being soaked in vinegar. 'Have you ever done that?' she asked.

'I think so, in school once maybe. It goes tight on your face, does it?'

'It falls off, like . . .' she searched for the word in the water, 'solder! Once it's dry it squeezes you then it kind of works its way off, you have to catch it before it falls. My mother worked in the hospital and from time to time she would sneak us rolls in her bag. We made lots, then some days after, when it was all dried, we would paint them.'

I twirled the mask around in my hand. 'You should do that now, could sell them too. Bet you could make one good as that.'

'That is factory-made. Plastic. Scott, when did we stop making things?'

'Cheaper to make in big batches.'

'No.' She looked at me, there was a cold whip of air from the sea, it pricked water in a film over her eyes the way sap wells in stems of flowers after I'd cut them. 'Children always work with their hands. When did we stop?'

'What about Perry's?'

'It's not the same thing,' she said. So much for lifting a shadow off.

'I don't know, just start making things again,' I told her.

'I might as well tell you, so you understand . . . I had two brothers, both younger, Oskar and Maciej. When Maciej was eighteen he took my father's police gun from under my parents' bed, and he shot himself, dead.'

'Your brother?'

'Yes, Scott. Now I am thinking about Maciej when I think about this poor man whose funeral you were at.'

I wondered if I should comfort her, but she seemed to be holding out well. I slid my hand on top of hers anyway, just in case it would help. 'I'm so sorry, Klaudia.'

She pulled her hand from under mine. Put it down by her side. She straightened up.

'I know. Everyone is sorry.'

A man walking his dog nodded at us as he passed.

'Evening,' I said. I thought about Klaudia. She was starting to open up, but it wasn't like Jasmine. Dribs and drabs of stuff that was open and closed. I wouldn't mention Mum when I knew Klaudia was a book that shut itself too quickly. I tried to keep it going while she was feeling like being serious. It's all I wanted, a conversation that meant something. I missed good meaty discussions that got my head all hot.

Our talks should do it for me, but they don't. No offence.

'Do you know why your brother . . . did it?'

'Like you say, Scott, we will never know why these things happen. Not really. Truly.'

I got the feeling there was plenty she could've told me if she'd wanted to, like me hiding my da away, just talking about Granny, that I'd went to university and had a long-term girlfriend there, that was the height of it.

Actually, calling Jasmine my girlfriend was laughable. For two and a half years we never went shopping together. Never went to parties, but we did always end up pulled together by the night's undertow, and on those days that Jasmine felt like bunking off class and lying in my bed. Truthfully, a lot of the times we didn't even shag, just lay skin to skin, telling each other things that were taboo. If she'd have been a girlfriend, I doubt then I would've told her any of the things.

Jasmine started telling me her stuff first, like how she used to shoplift in the Metro Centre, putting stuff inside her knickers. Put it this way, after our first kiss I should've counted my teeth.

Still, I trusted her. I told Jas about the time I went into my Granny's room, I so badly wanted money for a game for my Game Boy. My da had collected me. Taken me out for the day.

'Da, the class are going to see *Hamlet* in Belfast,' I said to him.

'Here we go, tapping me already,' he said. 'I don't have a bottomless pocket.'

'No.' I'd been dead defensive. 'Just telling you.' And I scuttled on indoors.

When it was two in the morning I crept into Granny's room. She usually kept her handbag on the dresser but I could see it, she'd fallen asleep with it in her arms. It was the upshot of having a son like my da. She was counting her teeth in her own way.

I tried to slip it away. It wouldn't come. I levered my fingers under the flap to feel for her purse. All I could find were tissues and sweet papers. Murray Mints. She was never without a bag. A wrapper rustled against my hand. She grabbed her bag tighter, groggily sat up.

'Who's there?' Granny asked, her voice furry.

'It's me, Granny.'

'Scott, what is it?' She looked round at her alarm clock, though she never needed it, always woke at five.

'It's Da,' I lied. 'I'm worried about him.'

'Ach, Scott, what'd he say?'

'I think he's back on the drink.' Billy Bullshitter.

'With your Da, you have to just hope he sees sense. Nothing you or I could say or do would help. Believe me, son, I've tried.'

'I know, I know,' I said.

'Go back to bed and don't worry about him.'

I told that to Jasmine, and in more depth. She knew all about Da too: the stabbings, prison. Jasmine still held her head on my chest. She didn't judge me then. Her skin felt so hot it was like her breasts, her thighs were melted stuck to me. Skin sticky and white as jasmine rice, as if she was named for the stuff.

She didn't flinch from me. Not Jas. All she said was: 'That's nothing. I've done far worse.'

12 April

From Jasmine I'd learnt my lesson. Knew not to develop those real strong feelings for anyone else ever again. Certain emotions don't look good on me, you see.

But despite all my attempts to cut myself off, a feeling managed to grow for Klaudia with next to no cultivation. It wasn't Jasmine-shaped, it was different, smaller. Far smaller. The type of feeling I found hard to put my finger on, pin down and say, I know you, you stupid feeling, floating against my ribcage. Now, would you do me the favour of kindly fucking away off?

No. With Klaudia it was spades and soil, bottle-green shorts and Perry's Nurseries polo shirts. And it was people, people interrupting us, Klaudia and me. I found people always interrupted the good stuff.

When she dropped me home after the lighthouse, Da nearly broke his bloody neck trying to look out of the window at us. At her. She insisted on sitting on, asking me if I was okay and me telling her I was sorry about her brother, again, if she ever needed someone to talk to that she could tell me anything . . . all that malarkey.

Klaudia leaned forward.

'Okay, I will let you into a secret,' she said, 'some nights I don't feel like brushing teeth.'

'But you do it anyway?'

'That is all you are getting.'

Klaudia laughed. She reached over and hugged me. In that split second Da worried himself into action around the dangers of passive smoking. He came outside with a feg in his hand and gave a little wave into the car.

'Who is that?' Klaudia asked.

'My da.'

'Your father?'

I nodded.

'He looks nice.'

'No he doesn't. Not one tiny bit.'

Klaudia gave him his wave back. I jumped out of the car, her little white Citroën AX, practically an antique, rusting holes around the wheel arches.

'See you soon,' I said.

'Of course. Any time you are off work, give me a buzz,' she said, miming a phone with her hand.

'That *our Klaudia*, I suppose?' Da asked me in the hall.

'Yep,' I said. I was in the kitchen where I was pouring myself a pint of milk to take up to bed with me. Da's trainers were tossing kicks in the washing machine drum.

Upstairs I checked my emails. Clint had sent a message to offer me work, starting the next day.

The job, well, that took up a couple of weeks. I had to knock back the Nurseries for once. Clint paid more. It was typical. Just when Klaudia was starting to confide in me, and I was eager to know more, we were kept apart. I had so many questions. It was all I could think about. I couldn't just text to ask her all the ins and outs.

But being a tree surgeon's assistant was lonelier than Perry's, with no customers to break up the tedium. Clint was the strong silent type, nose pressed to the grindstone.

Clint had done the job alone for so long that he had got out of the way of being remotely sociable, which was annoying because, if anything, he'd have had stories I actually would've wanted to hear. It's like people say, it's the quiet ones you have to watch. It's true, but not in any bad way. I'm not saying he was up to anything. Clint seemed like a stand-up guy. Well, he went to church but contrasted that with a bottle of vodka on a Friday night, he had four daughters 'all by the same woman' – he'd said that a couple of times like it was his unique selling point – and he'd never married his woman, which I suspect earned him some serious man points.

These are the things I gleaned from him, along with the odd technical tip about how to snip back ivy on the front of a house to a 'five o'clock shadow'. He said things like that. One day, after a rain shower, when I commented on the smell of the earth, Clint was able to tell me there was a name for it. It was called petrichor.

He was poetic in a way that far exceeded Pete Doherty's prowess. Clint was poetic the way people are when they work with nature properly. I don't count the Perry's lot in that. They may as well have worked in any shop. It was retail to them, and there's nothing poetic about retail. It's all about the small talk. The shit talk. And I was sick of that.

I used to be drawn to people because they seemed to wear their hearts on their sleeves, would just say anything for attention. Those types drew me in but pretty soon their loose tongues would let something slip that I'd be offended by. Or I'd be thinking that they were probably talking about me, seeing as how they spoke so freely and in the tiniest details about everything and everyone else.

That's why I like the quiet ones, because when they do crack, a whole array of the most interesting stuff comes seeping out.

19 April

The weeks after the funeral, working with Clint, I kept business hours, ate dinner with Da. A couple of the evenings he took himself off reeking of Joop for Men. It would've cut the throat out of you. I wouldn't give him the satisfaction of asking where he was going.

I stayed in one Saturday night in particular and the next morning I woke early, couldn't get back over. Light cut into the room from the small square window. There was clattering coming from someone opening and closing their car door. I got up, washed, dandered through the town.

There was a fuss at the rugby club. A car boot sale was being set up on the gravel car park. I got a cup of tea from a van selling fry-ups, sausage sodas, bacon-and-egg baps and hot drinks. The tea was orange. I mean, it was a styrofoam cup of pure unadulterated heartburn. I sat at a bench for a while trying to swallow it then gave up, poured it down the drain, threw the cup into a bin bag full of chippy wrappers.

I had a walk around. People were selling some pretty decent things for next to nothing and the skip divers were on form.

Callum had a little wallpaper-pasting table set up and the back of his Renault people carrier opened out, all the stuff his kids had grown out of in neat piles that kept getting messed up and strewn about. He rearranged the display and glanced up at me.

'Hiya, Scott. Thought I saw you walking through town recently.' He'd generally managed to avoid talking to me when we'd passed each other outside our homes, but now, away from our street, he was as friendly as you like. 'You done with university then?'

'Oh I'm done,' I said. 'And Da, you've probably seen him . . . he's moved in with me.'

'The bachelor pad, eh? That's great you're back. I mean, those lodgers liked a party. Now, I'm not sayin' . . . sure we were all young once. You *are* young, but you'd never get on like them two. Fellas coming and going at all hours. Bit much.'

I could just picture Aoife losing her shit with the lodgers. *See, in comparison I wasn't a bad neighbour to have, eh, Aoife?*

'Anything else in here?' asked one woman, swooping in to see what was in Callum's boot. She had a feg hanging out of her mouth as if it was stuck to her lip with glue, a little bearded pup at the end of the glittery pink lead which was resting in a loop in her hand.

'It's all out here,' Callum said.

'No women's clothes?'

'I'm not Marks & Spencer, love.' Then, in a sideline to me, 'See, I told Aoife that people would buy her old maternity junk. Maybe, next time . . .'

'What age are those jeans for?'

The woman's dog was up on its hind legs, sniffing round the clothes.

'Watch your dog,' Callum said, looking at the jeans in her hand. 'They're Diesel baby jeans. Three months. Designer. Get your dog off the clothes, please.'

He didn't mention her cigarette smoke though, I noticed. I'm always amused when people think one thing is bad, yet not the other. You'd have seen it on eBay and Gumtree: 'Item for sale comes from a smoke-free, pet-free home.'

'Item for sale comes from the home of one soulless fucker,' dope-fiend Farris once said. He was a smelly bastard and all, couldn't pass a dog in the street without mucking it about, getting it to roll over, him down on his knees rubbing those wee hairy teats. Him turning into a sap.

The woman shot Callum a look. 'Give you 50p,' she said.

Callum laughed. He looked at me now and tilted his head as if to say, *Listen to yer woman here.* 'Three quid? They cost twenty-five.'

'Twenty five! For a newborn baby's jeans? Somebody saw you coming!'

'Three quid.' He wasn't even looking at her by then.

'Go on, 50p for them, it's for a good cause, they're for my wee grandson.'

'No,' Callum told her, deciding she was wasting his time and so he could talk to me. 'Well, how's your gran doing?'

'Not bad. Going to see her later.'

Callum nodded, scratched his top lip with his bottom teeth, his jaw comically underslung. 'We'll have to have Mrs Mac round for tea some time.'

'She can't eat,' I said.

'Oh, I know, I know. I meant . . . we'll have to have her round just. Wee Mrs Mac, eh? We miss her about, you know?'

I'm sure you do, I thought, compared to my da. Granny let his kids get away with running through her garden. No, not garden, a tiny front yard with a wall they would sit on. It got Granny's goat but she was always too soft to say so. She was good to them. When Callum and his wife had their last kid, Granny knit loads of clothes, I remember her saying on the phone. It was just before she had her op and Da had her carted off. When I thought about it, I realised what the pile of blue woollen cardigans and hats in Callum's boot were.

'I've just had the snip,' Callum explained, as if he could read my thoughts, and he added, a bit too loudly if you ask me, 'Never do it, Scott. You never forget that smell of your tubes getting burnt. Fuck! Need rid of all this lot now the baby shop is shut. They're small, our style of house. For the five of us it's sardines.'

I could imagine. The only place I had to get away from Da was my room. Poky little shitboxes all right.

Callum had a box of DVDs, £1 each. I had a shuffle through.

'I've had my orders from Aoife. This is stuff I've had nearly as long as you've been alive, probably. No one watches DVDs anymore,' he said.

'No. I do,' I said, though I'd left mine in Newcastle, back when I thought I was being freed, before I knew I was being ensnared by counsellor McAuley.

Callum had the Matrix trilogy, *Braveheart*, *The Mummy* and some other shite: romcoms mainly, Jennifer Aniston's dire back catalogue. I lifted a handful, opened them to check they were in the right cases and not scratched. I handed over a fiver. Callum held it for a while as if he was maybe going to hand it back to me, then decided my money was as good as any other. He'd have something back for the independence he'd lost. I pictured him like Tony Soprano, heavy nasal breathing, *Hey, Aoife, stop burning my balls. I'll get rid of the DVDs, even if I have to have somebody whacked. Capiche?*

'Enjoy those.'

'I will,' I told him.

The woman with the dog was shouting now. She was going, 'Get away! Bad dog! Go on, shoo!' She had the feg in her hand now, though it was practically burnt all the way down, and the lead in the other hand. A bull terrier type was all around her scruffy wee mutt. Growling, her dog started snapping. Barking. The woman was going round in circles, hands held up delicately as if she was pegging the washing. Top-heavy in her knit jumper, she was. Massive tits on her and skinny little bird legs in a pair of black leggings.

'Throw the cigarette on the ground and lift your dog,' Callum told her, but she did neither, just shouting, circling as a crowd expanded around her.

'Fuck sake, who owns that dog?' someone was shouting.

'I don't know,' came multiple murmurs.

No one was wanting to do anything. The animal was getting more agitated.

'Get those kids out of the way, that thing is rabid,' an old woman said.

I got sick of the whole charade, set the DVDs down on the table and walked over and tweezed the cigarette out of her hand, her big sapphire ring scoring my hand. I stamped the feg into the gravel.

'Lift your dog!' I shouted in her face. 'Lift your fucking dog! Lift your fucking-rat-fucking-faced dog!'

She stared at me. Her dog whimpered. Everybody stared. A man in a Champion tracksuit came over, clipped his lead onto the other mutt and pulled him away, looking back at me like I was the mental one in the scenario.

'Wouldn't hurt a fly, calm yourselves down,' he said, just low enough for us to hear, but everyone was more focused on me than him.

'You all right, Scott, mate?' Callum asked me.

He was putting the DVDs into a carrier bag. He looked at

me the way nobody ever looked at me, until they did. Kyle and Farris had been the first, but it's the way people were starting to look at me more and more. That way everyone looks at me now. Like you do.

I snatched the bag from Callum. He patted me on the back as I walked off, feeling like my shoes were on the wrong feet. I went home and straight to my room.

First I meditated, then I set the DVDs out on my bed. I'd seen *The Matrix* before of course. Jesus – sure it's a classic. When I was younger I used to write fan fiction about it. I'd take the characters past the film and see where they'd go. I hadn't done it in so long, I kept it for another time.

I'd never seen *The Mummy*. Even the name of it, *The Mummy* – it sounds like a young kids' film. I wondered why Callum hadn't just kept it for his boys. I watched it on my laptop. A slow starter, like anything that had aged. Like watching cartoons that Granny would've said, 'Your Da liked that,' way before the man had any putrid associations for me.

I had wanted to like anything that my da did, so that I could tell him when I was finally able to visit him in 'hospital'. I'd sit, watch, hear the canned laughter, think, *In the name of God how did people watch this guff?* Everything seemed in slow-mo and surrounded by old biddies.

The Pumpkins have this song. 'Disarm', you call it. It's a cracker. It's about a little boy being old in his shoes. See? Billy Corgan, now he understands me.

Anyway, *The Mummy* would've been a scary enough film for kids, thinking back. I never watched anything like it being raised by Granny. She liked antiquated films, as you can imagine. James Stewart. That kind of thing.

Every Christmas we watched *It's a Wonderful Life*. Even

when I was home from uni, the Christmas before the last one, a couple of months before Da came and got me, we sat in her little apartment in the fold and watched it together.

What is it you want, Mary? What do you want? You want the moon? Just say the word and I'll throw a lasso around it and pull it down. Hey. That's a pretty good idea. I'll give you the moon, Mary.

That's the one scene that makes the whole movie worth watching.

Our last Christmas all together – all three of us McAuleys together, I mean – it dawned on me that Da had played down the seriousness of Granny's illness all along. She couldn't eat any Christmas dinner. It was a sin, really.

'Your granny needs an operation, the nurses have arranged somewhere for her to stay, she needs care,' he'd told me, via a text or two. Not one for calls, not even in emergencies. And if your granny having tracheal cancer wasn't an emergency, I don't know what qualified.

Historically, Christmas was always a nice time with Da. He was all right when I remember back, when he was just in small doses, like eye drops. It'd sting a bit but then everything would fizz and soon your brain was telling you this was normal. It wouldn't last. *Normal vision returning soon.*

Granny would've made everything from scratch in the past, kicking proceedings off months before by steeping dried fruit in booze for the Christmas pud. I remember that great prep, those final touches. Every year Granny made me my own nut roast, so that when it was just her and me left having the remains on Boxing Day – and Da scampered away off again with a foil-covered platter for his fridge in a kitchen I never got to see, was never invited to see – she'd have sat over another plate of turkey, and I'd have had the balance of my roast in peace and quiet.

Boxing Day was usually better than Christmas, to be truthful. At Christmas we used to sit around the kitchen table with our paper hats rustling. Da was the main instigator for that, he'd be going on about us 'two bores'. Just showed up, he did, to show us up. Having the fun but none of the work. That's if he was even having fun. It was probably all he could to do to blast through the house and keep up a jolly smile, keep the Troubles talk to a minimum. He had more respect than to have my granny hear all that.

All the talk about his fellas was stored up for me, for when one of the fellas 'unavoidably' attempted to kill himself in prison on New Year's Eve – suicide did a brisk trade then too, it wasn't just a thing kept for spring – and Da never showed up to our 'parties'. Though we never claimed they were ever going to be worthy of the title 'party'. Not in years had we called anything a 'party'.

He'd just text me his apologies every time anyway. So it was just Granny and I, drinking Babychams straight from squat green bottles, scoffing Bombay Mix from the bag burrowed in the sofa cushions between us. Both of us analysing the running order on Jools Holland's *Hootenanny*, how it was getting worse with every year. But that was a couple of years ago now.

But the Christmas after Granny's operation was different from all the others. After her operation she stayed in the fold. It would've upset her too much to invite her back to her own house, Da reckoned. So we were to go to her. Bring the mountain to Mohammed. Da had been texting me, you see, to say, 'Your granny loves making Christmas dinner sure.'

'I don't think we should expect her to anymore,' I texted back, standing outside my lecture, turning my phone to silent in those long, desolate days when Jasmine was getting over less and less.

'Will you get the stuff? I'll reimburse you,' Da had text.

'I'll not be home till Xmas Eve.'

'Fine. I'll get a food delivery. Not going near the shops, everyone's acting the fuckin lig!'

That's what we did. He got the stuff from 'the Tescos' and fired it into Granny's oven in the fold. Da forgot all the trimmings: no cranberry sauce, no gravy even. Granny had to go to Deedee in the room down by the reception to ask if she had anything to help lube the dried-bark turkey.

Deedee's family lived in Canada and her nephew, who was supposed to have her over for Christmas dinner, had cancelled at the last minute. So along Deedee came, Bisto chicken gravy granules in hand, and she was quickly, and all too easily, persuaded to eat with us.

You couldn't blame her. But I'm not complaining, Deedee stopped Christmas being about Da. He'd bought a tiny turkey that barely fed the two of them, them that did eat, and ate meat: Deedee and himself.

'Christ, that was dear for all we got. I thought it was going to be massive,' Da said.

He tried to slide a slice onto my plate.

'I'm a vegetarian, Da,' I said.

'Ah, your nut roast,' Granny said, hand clamped to her forehead to emphasise she'd forgotten.

'I'll roast his nuts for him, bringing nothing along,' Da said.

'It's okay, Granny,' I said, ignoring him.

Granny was sitting in that shoebox. *There was an old woman who lived in a shoebox, she had so few children she didn't know what to do, and the one she had was a cunt.*

Of course she wasn't missing anything worth writing home

Kelly Creighton

about by not eating, but she seemed bloody pitiful. We sat crammed around her little breakfast bar until Da said, 'Let's just get trays and sit in the lounge.'

Granny only had one tray, so Deedee, Da and I had our dinner plates on tea towels on our laps. I ate the potatoes mashed, lumpy as they'd been in the bag, no variation, no roasties fried in oil. I could've done better. Cooked a bit. Only I hadn't thought.

Maybe I should've taken charge, but instead I chewed my spongy spuds and watched Granny sitting, looking all around with a hamster-ish expression. She loved Christmas dinner. I could see it nearly killed her. She had no motivation to make it nice for us, and why should she? She deserved a year off. For Chrissake she'd been sick and was living there. We should've pulled together, me and Da, should've been better organised, shown her that we could do it, that we weren't relying on her to hold everything together anymore, that she could sit back now, and even if she couldn't eat it she could see *us* enjoy *our* dinner.

That's what annoyed me; we never tried to make *her* have a nice Christmas. We didn't think about the pleasure she took from other people's enjoyment. But sure, you can't go back. There's no point in tormenting yourself with these things. Even though it's all I do sometimes. And the days are endless in here.

'Enjoying your spuds, Scott?' Da had asked,

'Ah for dear sake, give that boy of yours a break,' Deedee said. It was one of the things you didn't say to Duke McAuley, he may have lightened at Christmas – so to speak, and so it seemed – but it was still always eggshell-treading with him.

'How long have you lived in the fold, Deedee?' I asked her.

'Three years now, son,' she said. 'Took a bit of convincing to leave there but it's a nice crowd, here.' She pointed her fork at the floor.

'Here . . .' That's how Da starts conversation, says 'here' so you look at him, so you think he's going to give you something. Then he takes it away with the rest of his words: he's a thief, you always feel robbed of something after talking to him.

'Here, they've a hairdressers and everything,' Da hooted. 'It's a geg!'

People like me get narked by his sarcasm, but older people don't care one wee bit. I wonder if I'll ever stop.

'We have outings and socials,' Granny said. She was smiling at Deedee. 'I'd have asked you in for your dinner, you should've said about your nephew cancelling on you.'

'Ah, their wee one has come out with a rash, can't lift his head up, they're away to A & E.'

'Meningitis?' asked Da.

'Don't know, son. Hope not,' Deedee said. She looked apprehensive.

There was silence for ages then. We all picked at our food while Granny looked at the cracker booty from under the soft pleats of her eyelids.

'Unbelievable the things you get in crackers nowadays.'

She held the tiny deck of playing cards, the tape measure. I didn't know what she meant. It was always the same old tat since I could ever remember: tiny sewing kit, miniature slinky. Maybe it was the quality she meant.

'The jokes are always shite but,' Da said.

'Read one, son,' Deedee said. 'I didn't bring my glasses, be a dear.'

Da unravelled a white paper rectangle from its coiled position.

'Right,' he said 'What do you call it when Santa has a sore throat?'

He followed it up with a big phlegmy sniff.

I felt like someone had dragged my chair out of the room, like I was watching something I wasn't a part of. Everything was so small. It was like claustrophobia. Like my brain made the walls melt away so I'd stop feeling like I was sitting in a doll's house.

Granny and Deedee looked at each other, they shook their heads.

'Isla, do you know?' Deedee asked Granny.

'No, I haven't heard this one before . . . Santa with a sore throat.'

Her finger came up to her chin. I could almost see a question mark draw itself over her head. When her head lifted like that you could see her stoma, make out the rope of scar on her throat, glinting like silk against the light of the TV.

The queen was delivering her speech on silent. 'Let's watch the queen's Christmas message,' always meant just that: watch but don't listen. Her plummy voice was a distraction, and we'd heard Da's impressions too many times before, his usual, 'Will she mention Diana this year?' Diana was to the queen – in his head – what the Troubles were to 'the big guys' in Stormont.

'Isla, come on, think,' Deedee said.

Their two faces were as serious as you could ever see two faces, still pondering Santa's sore throat, though you'd have thought they were on *University Challenge*, being asked who preceded the Marxist agenda in Germany in 1934 . . . or something to that effect.

'No?' Da asked, bobbing his head at each one of us. 'Will I just tell you? Scott, you want to hazard a guess? You want to phone a friend? Do you want to phone someone first and ask if they'll be your friend?'

I knew it was 'tinsel-it is'. Put me out of my misery, I felt like saying.

'No idea,' I said.

'Tinsel-itis,' Da said.

I must've heard that joke every year, but why spoil the fun of the chase for the ladies.

'Jesus, tinsel-itis,' Da said. 'Fuck sake.'

'Language, Edward,' Deedee said.

Da looked amused, lips disappearing in wonder that some-one had managed to chastise him. He was quiet for a while. No one called him Edward, only Granny. I could tell Granny would want Deedee there for every visit Da gave thereafter.

Granny fussed over me for a while – had I had my flu jab?

'It doesn't give you flu,' she told me.

'No,' and, 'I know,' were my responses.

'Are you still not registered with a doctor over there?' she asked, doing little stretchy movements with her spine as she talked. Like a little bird, she is.

'No.'

'For dear sake, Scott!'

'Stop bloody fussing, Ma,' Da said. It was taking the atten-tion off him. 'Well, Deedee, what did the man in red bring you? Have you been a good girl?' Da asked her, shiny side up again.

She giggled. 'I haven't been a girl in many a moon. I'll take that for a Christmas present, you saying that. Girl!' She put down her fork diagonally across her plate. 'My son in Vancouver sent me vouchers. The grandkiddies made a video, they've put a card in the post but it must be late. My son isn't good with the times, he sends stuff too late all the time. Only reason I have my voucher was because it got sent from here: House of Frazer, he bought it on the computer.'

'Oh, that's lovely.' Granny squeezed Deedee's hand. 'You can treat yourself.'

'I will Isla, but what I really want is an antique bookcase I saw recently.'

'Oh yeah?' Da looked up at Deedee, a smidge of a frown settling on him. 'A reader, are you?'

'Listen, son, I've hundreds of books.' She arced her hand in a swift wave.

'Where d'you keep them all?'

'They're all in boxes in my bedroom. They're a damn pain to get round. I've been saving and I saw that bookcase and fell in love . . . but I'd no way of getting it home.'

'You can hire vans now,' Da said.

I shot him a look. She could barely walk, let alone drive a van. And lug it up one flight of stairs too. *Asshole*.

'I could-n't a-ffor-d it,' Deedee's voice made separate words of every syllable when she spoke like that. Hopeless, like.

'That's how they get you, Deedee,' Granny said.

'I don't like feeling got,' Deedee told her.

'Nobody does,' I said.

Da looked at me. He sat back and rubbed his hands on his trousers, those suit trousers for funerals, Christmas and accompanying sons to uni interviews. He flicked his finger in her direction. 'I'll get it for you Deedee, you tell me where . . . and I'll get it for you.'

'Do you have a van, Edward, son?'

'No, I don't, but I'll borrow one. I have this mate . . .' he started.

You don't need to hear the rest of that. He started to ramble about someone he knew, shoehorning in the counselling, because he hadn't mentioned it since we'd sat down.

'Oh, you're a dear,' Deedee said. She got up and kissed him on the top of his silver head. 'Isla, your son is a gentleman. A gen-til-man.'

Granny had a hint of a smile. 'Wasn't this a lovely Christmas? We should do it again next year,' she said.

'Next time with the trimmings though,' I said.

'Yes, next year, if God spares us all,' Granny said.

Deedee gave a sharp intake of breath. 'Oh, no, I hate that expression.'

The nurse knocked at the door, let herself in, threw her shadow on the magnolia-painted wall. She was wearing a Santa hat, a red coat pulled over her uniform, the coat two sizes too small – like the Grinch's heart – pushing her chest up so it was nearly a shelf for her chin. It certainly looked like Christmas had come for my da by the dumb bake on him.

'Everybody okay in here? Oh, Deedee, there you are.'

'We're having a family dinner, Becca.'

Nurse Becca painted a too-pleased look on her face. Bit phony.

'We're having a bit of entertainment in the Green Room later, are you sticking around for it, lads?' she asked.

'Will there be mistletoe?' Da asked her.

'Oh flip! Where'd you get this one, Isla?' asked Becca, a new start at the fold – they changed staff there quicker than they changed the old dears' knickers.

Becca didn't know my da was an aggravating customer for the most part, telling the workers that he worked with prisoners and that the old folk in the fold were treated worse than prisoners, which I thought at the time was absolute shite. And now I *know* it's shite.

Nurse Becca peeked over everybody.

'You need your lactulose, Deedee? That might be a bit rich for you,' she said, one hand on her meds trolley stoppering the door open.

'I went this morning, a good big one, would've made this big fella proud if he'd have done it.'

She meant Da.

He put his fork down.

'Happy Christmas,' the nurse said, backing out of the door, as excited as if Narnia was on the other side.

'To you, too,' everyone said, bar Da.

He said nothing. He took a drink of Shloer instead: Shloer was as hard as the drink got for him.

'Anybody for coffee?' Granny asked.

'Me,' Da said. *Me. Me. Me.*

Granny stood up and got the cups ready with a dribble of milk in the bottom.

'Got any green tea, Granny?' I asked her.

Da was visibly in pain by the question.

'No, love.'

The air in her throat beat like a door not properly closed. She pottered about with the cups in her new cupboard, in her new home.

20 April

Da was driving me back to the house from the fold. It hit me hard, seeing Granny totally removed from everything. I tried to force some words out, but all I could think to say was, 'Deedee's delighted about that bookcase.'

She'd grabbed him into a hug, pressed a grateful kiss into his neck before we left.

'You can give me a hand with it. Hopefully your granny won't want one too. She can't see green cheese—'

He stopped.

'What's that?'

I pretended I wasn't listening fully, but I wanted to hear what he had to say. I'd seen no exchange of gifts.

I'd given Granny the pamper-hamper I'd filled half a suitcase with. Jasmine had helped me make it up: bath salts, candles, stuff I never knew if Granny would appreciate. Stuff Jasmine insisted she would. She tea-leafed most of it for me – I didn't ask her to. She said Granny would probably never buy herself fancy things but she'd be glad of the thought, that all women want to be spoiled with little luxuries. Granny couldn't eat or drink anymore so we – yes, sweet that Jasmine said 'we'! – had to be creative.

Jas would've loved it if someone had made her something as thoughtful, she'd said, and Granny had liked it, as far as I could tell. She had smiled and hugged me the same as any year. Maybe it was the tubes and the surroundings that gave everything that spike of depression it shouldn't have had, because, after all, the fold apartment *was* beautifully kitted out compared to the house: fresh paint, modern kitchenette, everything brand-spanking new and shiny. But still, that kernel of regret buried deep in my chest was there, so much so that I only went a handful of times.

I did to Granny what Da did for years: I steered clear. When we did meet up we went for a walk around the commons, or sometimes she came with a carer to see me at the Nurseries, but we kept our distance from each other's homes. Mine was filled with memories and the reminder that she had had her choices stripped from her, and hers, to me, was filled with what happens to you when your liberty is taken.

I tried my best to run from it, but it's a part of life that catches up with you and gets you in its grasp. It says try all you want, there are things you cannot escape, ever.

'What did *you* get Granny for Christmas?' I asked Da.

'Same as she got me,' Da said, spitting a chewed up fingernail into the footwell.

'What's that?'

'Sweet Fanny Adams,' Da said. 'We agreed it's pointless. Sure it's giving to receive, cancelling each other out. We aren't children.'

You are, I felt like saying, you're the biggest child I've ever seen. I had to dig at him, I couldn't let it go. I didn't care if I went back to Newcastle in the bad books. He was the main subject of mine.

'Da, could you not have got Granny *something*? She seemed excited about Deedee's bookcase.' *Stir, stir, stir.* 'Maybe you should surprise her. She deserves something after everything she's been through.'

'We've all been through shit,' Da said. 'What room do they have for bookcases, fuck sake? Your granny's got about five books anyway, and they're all tripe!' said the man who didn't know who William Shakespeare was. *You're going to see Hamlet. Wha', the cigar? William? Oh, you mean Billy! Billy Shakespeare, lives off Circular Road?*

That reminds me of this one time he was talking about a man he knew in Belfast, a rabbi whose brother was a moneylender.

'A Jewish moneylender? Like Shylock?' I'd asked his blank face – I liked *that* face! – and he had just frowned. '*The Merchant of Venice*,' I'd added on, as if that should help. But Da glossed over with something else. A paint he knew the colour of.

'Why don't you buy Granny a nice lamp or something then? Women like to be spoiled.'

I blame Jasmine for that last remark. I *was* being a copycat *then*. Her little ways had rubbed off onto me.

'You going to tell *me* about women?' Da was rightly amused. He was able to slide it right off him onto me like an insignificant crumb. 'You got a girl in uni?'

'What if I do?'

'Listen, Scott, there are a few of my fellas have come out as gay, you know? Just sayin'. It's nearly 2013.'

'I'm not gay,' I told him.

'It'd be all right if you were. Me and your granny would accept you the same.'

Aye, and this is the level his acceptance would've reached: just about the Sweet Fanny Adams mark. The same indeed. I didn't say anything. If he wanted to tell himself I was homosexual then let him. Fine by me.

Da looked at the snowman in Callum's front yard and pulled his mouth like he was shifting something between his teeth with his tongue.

'Here, Scott, what's the difference between a snowman and a snow woman?' he asked.

I smiled at him, through teeth sore from being gritted more than the roads in town.

'Snow balls,' he said. 'Get it?'

'Got it.'

We sat in the car a while, both thinking about what to say next. How to wrap the day up.

'Hope Deedee's nephew enjoyed his dinner in peace. I'll have to remember that excuse in future,' Da said. 'That *rash* one,' he added, looking at my confused face. Then I remembered.

'Oh, yeah. The rash.'

'Rash my left bollock!' said Da.

There was no point saying anything, was there? Some child psychologist once reckoned that when you get to seven years old you are already who you are going to turn out to be when you are an adult. By that token I left Da alone. You can't teach an old dog new tricks and all that. Is there any point trying to sway anybody's mind when they get to a certain stage of life? I wouldn't have thought so.

It's ingrained in us, who we are. DNA, the swirls of our fingerprints, they are us, solely. Unchanging. I know what you're thinking: I could've told him that was a callous, terrible thing to accuse Deedee's nephew of. But, do you know what? He could've been right.

People *are* selfish. They want what they want and they want to shirk off the things that tie them down. We're lazy. We're all guilty. Okay, you go on believing that you aren't. I think if you were more honest, even just with yourself, you'd agree.

I got out of the car. He headed back to Belfast. The house was mine and mine alone until I had to get back to Newcastle to start the new term.

5 May

'Come on, I'll catch you. Promise I won't let anything bad happen.'

'No, Mummy.'

'Scott, don't be afraid, I'm here.'

She put her arms out for me. The sun was shining on her face in the park that day, so it was hard to make it out, but that could be the way time changes things, makes them fuzzed and faceless, leaving us to fill in the gaps.

The few photos that we had showed Mum as dimensionless. They're what I struggle with. I know what she looked like, in one or two stances, on one or two occasions, but standing in front of me, arms out, waiting for me to fall into them . . . I have to reconstruct that. It's like putting on 3D glasses to make her pop up from the flat of my mind.

Granny had three photos of Mum: one of her and Da with Granny on their wedding day, though you couldn't tell it was a wedding. They are in trouser suits, even Mum. She had a curly perm that I never knew her with.

There is one, too, of her holding me in the hospital when I was just born. Mum's looking at me. The blanket is up over my mouth – it looks that way anyway – and a blue hat is nearly covering my eyes. There is just a lot of sheet. Blank, white origami folds. Mum's face is turned sideways. So pale, it is. Her green eyes almost closed.

I hate that photo. I used to turn it round the other way or set it face down for years, but Granny never took the hint. Mum has her mouth shut in a smile that looks knowing, in a way, sad that she maybe knew we had so little time, but of course she couldn't have.

Then there's the one of me on my third birthday. Mum is just a figure in the background. You can see the back of Mrs Wright, the woman who lived in the terrace next door to us. I think it's her, although I have no idea what age of a woman Mrs Wright was. Something tells me she was old but when I looked at that photo I think she was maybe young like my mum, who was only twenty years old when she died. One year younger than I am now.

That day in particular, in the park, stands out: the cold of the climbing-frame bar against my cheek, Mum having to lift me down because I'd lost my nerve. Maybe every day was like that, me deciding to go for something then bottling out halfway through. Sounds like the old me all right.

'Let's get home and have a cup of tea.' Mum beckoned me with her hand.

I remember things like that. I remember I used to drink cooled-down tea in a tommee tippee, loaded with sugar. Cold tea out of a plastic mouthpiece. The smell of tea with sugar in it brings it back to me.

That was our routine: walk to the newsagent's to do some shopping, walk to the park to have a play about, then home again for a cup of tea and watch some TV, just me and Mum, nobody visiting much.

Granny had moved to town the year Da got put away, and Mum only had one brother. He lives in England – Nottingham or Birmingham – and he never bothered with her when she was living. I can't remember if he was at the funeral, I just remember getting loads of attention, feeling like people were going to wear a hole in my head from patting my hair. And I remember getting the giggles at all the people crammed into our living room and going hysterical when they played her favourite song. (I can't tell you what it is. I do remember, but when I hear it on the radio I turn it over or off. I don't like to think about it. It was a big track too. Not one that gets lost in time, heaped over with new soil of new tunes. No. This one shows no sign of leaving.)

Birmingham. It was Birmingham, now I think about, where Mum's brother lives. I remember because a few years ago he took a notion that he wanted to get in touch with me. He wrote for about five months, telling me how he was doing in work in a mechanic's yard, how he supported West Brom – that's right – and how I should come over and he'd take me out to a match. But I was too honest, saying, 'I've no interest in football,' and then it became apparent how little we had in common, except that he once spent nine months in a womb which was later the same womb that made the person whose womb I underdeveloped in for a portion of that time. See how abstract the notion family really is?

He wrote to me at one stage too, Mum's brother, saying how he'd met a nice girl in a bar. She was his mate from work's cousin or something. Some vague linkage. He was going to ask her out. He had no luck with the ladies, he said, made some joke about how they always smelt him coming. His interest in me waned. The wanting to reach out to his only living family fizzled. Ned, you called him.

I wonder if Ned's heard about me on the news.

Hold on, I'm being summoned. I'll finish this later.

★

One morning Mum disappeared into the kitchen – more like mid-morning actually. She fetched me a bowl of dry cereal and lay up on the sofa. I'd already had my cereal but she said, 'This will tide you over, Scott, the last of the cereal. We'll get some later when we go out.'

I'm not pretending I completely remember every wee detail, but it feels that way. I mean, how much of any account is really accurate? After all, my life didn't happen to me in sentences. It happened in the silences.

Of course I realise my mind has filled in the blanks. What I don't know, I've been told, or I've read. So bear with me, because it's all true either way – the bones of it.

Mum had her dressing gown on, a shiny quilted thing covered in stitched diamonds. She lifted me on up the sofa and set me on her knee, put her cheek on my head and wrapped her arms around me, saying that we would give the park a miss that day, that outside it looked like it was going to piddle down.

I looked outside. It was grey, right enough. The day was finding itself stuck in the dregs of winter light. March was sitting in, waiting for spring to knock on the door.

Mum got up and pulled the curtains shut again, as if we were going to start our morning again, in a while. 'A wee minute,' she said. She just needed a bit more time to get herself going.

'You want to put on a video?' Mum asked.

I jumped down and ran to the TV in the corner of the room. I lifted my video, shuffled it out of its cover. Santa had brought me one of Barney, this big purple dinosaur that was my favourite then. Mrs Wright had stood laughing at it when she'd see it.

'My God, thon thing's wired up,' she said about him.

I love you, you love me, we're a happy family.

'Kids love it,' Mum told her.

'Whoever wrote this must've been having a wee puff beforehand,' I can hear Mrs Wright saying.

Mum would've roared with laughter. I'd have been delighted they were watching too, that they found it as hypnotic as I did.

I slid the video into the player and went back to sit on top of Mum, eat my dry cornflakes from the bowl, no spoon, just fingers.

'Again, again,' I said when Barney prepared to sing the song. I knew it off by heart.

'You smart boy,' Mum said.

'Cuppa tea?' I asked her.

'In a wee minute, love.'

Her fingers kept disappearing into the hair on the left side of her head, her eyes screwing themselves shut tight, mouth grimacing. After a while – it could've been half an episode or four of them, the whole length of the tape – Mum spilt me off her onto the sofa.

'Mummy?' I called but she didn't answer. I continued watching and crunching cornflakes with my back teeth, grinding little golden shards.

I thought she was going upstairs to get my clothes. I heard a thump. I didn't go to look for a while. When I did, Mum was laying on the stairs, near the bottom of them, head first, as if she'd leapt into a pool from a diving board.

Mum's arms were twisted behind her back and her hands were poking out, one bent all the way back like it should've hurt her. Her face was covered with her chestnut hair.

'Mummy?' I asked, shaking her shoulders.

She moved but stayed were she was. I gave up, I knew how the tape rewound itself, it was easy, I didn't need to remember which button to press, if I let it go right to the end it would rewind itself. Start again. Mum had shown me how.

The screen was blank for a long time so I played with my kitchen then: stirred pots, got my little plastic pot and poured a cup of pretend tea for Mum. I went out to the stair and set it beside her.

'Mummy, cuppa tea for you,' I said, lifting her hair and peeking under it.

It was cut to her shoulders. Splayed out. Her eyes stared at the wall. *She's awake*, I thought. I went back to get her a plate which was all cracked under the varnish of it, like it could fall apart in your hand. I put a slice of pretend cake on it. She liked Bakewell tarts best. I pretended to put a cherry on the top and lifted a spoon too, for stirring her tea and eating her cake.

Was it a game? But when we played hide-and-seek together she always hid in the same place. Always under my bed. Maybe she'd asked me to find her and I'd been distracted by Barney. But I had found her, and she was still being still. Still not talking.

Sometimes she did that, on the sofa. When I was passing she'd grab me out of the blue and tussle me into a cuddle, plant kisses all over my face, tell me I was her best wee mate. *Love you, Kiddo*.

I pulled at her hands, they were cold and white. *So* white. I wasn't scared then because the whole house was cold, that's why we were wearing our dressing gowns, see? I slid beside the wall so that she was looking at me.

'Found you, Mummy.' I laughed.

Found you, like it was a song or something, like a fucking simpleton.

I went back into the living room. That whirring sound video players made was starting up, whipping up a storm in the corner. I sat and watched it God knows how many times. Later I had a peek at her. She hadn't moved. She wasn't going to move, but for some reason I kept expecting Mum to sit up and say, 'Gotcha!' Grab me. Tickle the life out of me.

I got hungry. The cereal box was empty. That's how we lived – little by little. There was no such thing as a stocked larder or a full fridge. And I think this is why: there were times when mates of Da's would come round and try to give her envelopes that I only realised later had money in them, but Mum always refused them.

'No, I'm not starting trouble,' I'd heard her say one time when this one guy came round with a present for me too.

I knew it was for me because of the paper: blue with cartoon cars zooming over it, little puffs of smoke farting out the back of them.

'While Duke's waiting to get out take these,' the guy said.

'Give them to somebody else, we've got enough. Scott wants for nothing,' she said, which was truer there than any other time in my life.

When I think about the toys I had, I'm not sure whether

they were second-hand – I doubt it – or whether she saved up or even got herself into debt to get them for me. But she always made sure I had everything. She had nothing. The house wasn't great. I can tell that from the photo of my party. But *I* had everything.

I wonder how things would've turned out if she hadn't died, but there's no use, maybe she'd have taken him back and he'd have ruined her in some different way. I'll always picture Mum as perfect. But maybe we should never look back.

I think it was likely that she bought some supplies every day to keep her sociable and to give me a routine.

'You can take your Scott anywhere,' Mrs Wright often said, and Mum would beam from ear to ear.

I was getting thirsty. I knew Mum said the only tea little boys could make was pretend tea. I could see that the glass milk bottle was empty anyway. It sat on the counter on top of its own white halo. I pulled the chair over to the sink, poured water from the tap into my beaker. It blasted so hard it splashed the floor, the counter, my arms and my face. I tried to turn it off but it wouldn't go. I tried to put the lid back on my beaker with two hands pressing down, but the whole thing toppled and water went all over and dribbled onto the floor. I gave it up as a bad job.

Later I was so hungry I ate what I now know were Oxo cubes. Despite the shiny wrapper and looking like chocolates, they were foul. I wiped them off my tongue with a tea towel but the taste wouldn't leave. Then there was the pasta, dried yellowish swirls of it in a plastic bag. I took one out and ate it. It was a lot crunchier than cornflakes. It stuck in my throat.

I went to sleep beside Mum on the stairs until I awoke freezing. Mum was freezing, and I was uncomfortable, trying to curl myself around the bend of the stair. I went into Mum's bed, where she generally let me sleep with her even though I had a big boy's bed now and my bedroom was all decorated in Fireman Sam to entice me in. Because people like Granny and Mrs Wright said Mum would never get me out of her bed. But Mum didn't listen to them, it was our secret.

'With a great big hug and a kiss from me to you, please say that you love me too.' Our bedtime prayer, straight from the book of Barney. I sang that alone. I slept on her side so I could smell her lavender bed spray, which clung to her like perfume.

In the morning, daylight leaked into her bedroom then filled the room with sour yellow. The curtains were still separated from one another and Mum had not come to her side of the bed. When I stood at the top of the stairs I saw her at the bottom, an indoor river almost wetting her hair, then I started to scream. I screamed and screamed and screamed until I saw the front door burst through and the river drain out into the front yard.

Mr Wright came in and lifted Mum. He was crying that cry people call 'breaking your heart'. 'My Trevor *broke his heart* when he found Mandy dead on the stairs,' Mrs Wright told Granny when she made her way from the town to the Wrights' wee kitchen in the city.

Mrs Wright and another neighbour I don't remember the name of tread up the stairs and lifted me into the Wrights' house, where I screamed even more for Mum. They told me to shush, they tried to hug me, but I held my arms against my sides. My nose bled with the pressure inside my head.

They looked at each other. One of them said, 'Poor child doesn't have a clue what's just happened.'

The other said, 'What are they going to do with him now?'

4 June

When Da started offering to collect me after some of my shifts at the Nurseries I knew he just wanted to see 'the girl who phones you', as he called Klaudia. He'd made himself known to the staff, had come in and bought a bar of chocolate just to get the chance to give them all the is-Scott-behaving-himself business, spouting: 'Don't leave your car keys lying around with him about, for dear sake.'

Thankfully, every one of my colleagues laughed him off, but Da knew what he was doing. That eejit knew all right. After a few attempts to embarrass the hell out of me, he took the hint and left me to walk home, which was just as well because Klaudia was never about either. There were signs about her. There were usually signs everywhere about everything, and for some reason I always refused to see them.

Klaudia used to text me all the time. She told me to contact her anytime. I was going to ask more about her brother Maciej, why he did himself in and all of that craic, but all of a sudden she dropped off the radar. I didn't see Klaudia again for ages. Even when Clint didn't need me anymore Klaudia never had a shift at the same time as me. Although we couldn't work it out to meet up, she would still reply to my messages, even sent through a few job applications. Kept it short and sweet, putting notes in the emails like, 'You are worth more than a few shifts here and there. You are smart, Scott. I think this would suit you.' Things like that.

Then, one day, when she told me she'd be working, I called in. But Klaudia never showed. The text I sent to ask her why she'd lied, she ignored. And the next one.

Finally, she sent me a message, said that she'd been told she was working, then, an hour before she was to come in, she received a call to tell her that there'd been a mistake. I'd been in the tea room-cum-office, looking at my phone, sitting with Hugo while he took his dinner break. I was feigning an interest while he chatted about Spain, about how his wife wanted them to move there. So I know Hugo didn't call Klaudia. No one did. She downright lied.

'Was there something in particular you want to talk about?' she asked, and I felt sick. It wasn't like her, not the Klaudia I'd come to know. Come to hope that I could trust.

'When can we meet?' I asked her.

'I'm really busy at the moment.'

She was doing an online course. Animal psychology. She'd received a money-off voucher on one of those Groupon sites, she said, but for someone who was supposed to be on the computer a lot she never seemed to look at her emails.

In work there was a notice on the board, a permanent job was going. The details were: shift work, flexible hours, weekends and evenings.

'Is that for here?' I asked Hugo, as he strained over the lid of soup poured from his flask. His face was bulbous, nose-heavy, like it was looking at you from the back of a spoon.

'It is, aye,' he said. 'Looking for someone full-time. Know anyone who might be interested?'

'Well . . . me,' I said.

'Ah-ha?' he said, blowing on his soup, lifting the lid to slurp at it.

'Think I might,' I said.

I'd be pretty pissed off with myself if I did that just to get to see Klaudia again. If I was doing it just to gage how she was around me, I'd say to myself, 'Get a life!' But I didn't have a life.

84

When you don't have bigger things in your life, the small things become magnified. Things were magnifying.

Why was Klaudia blanking me? It plagued my mind like you wouldn't believe. If I'd been in love with Klaudia, or even fancied her more than the tiny bit that I did, then it would've made sense, but it didn't, like everything else in my life.

No part of me seemed in sync with the rest. It started to surprise me that I'd ever sat in lecture theatres and learnt about histories and theologies when I couldn't even keep the basics in my head without them spilling back out of my ears.

I began to keep a notepad. I thought it would help. One of the mummy types in the Nurseries walked past me one shift. I don't know her name, never bothered to find out. They all seem the same to me, almost as bad as the old biddies and the old boys who all seemed to merge into the same person. I felt like Klaudia and I gravitated to each other because we were the two different types. I was the young buck and she was the hot foreigner the old lads like Hugo fawned over in work, hands on her shoulder when they were talking. She was the truffle under the pigs' noses.

This woman, however, was not a different type of person, she was a frumpy mummy, the type that called herself a 'yummy-mummy', but was as yummy as a bowl of uncooked minced beef. She stopped at a stand, this woman, one of the few times I was on till duty. I was young, gaining weight, getting muscular from heaving boxes about the place. I had a lifestyle that was so clean it was almost transparent.

I can't remember why I was on the till that day. Maybe someone was on their lunch break or their smoke break. But this crummy-mummy – Stacey, we'll call her – was looking at embroidered notebooks. They were in Chinese, silk-look covers.

'They're new. Bet they're a rip-off, Perry knows how to price things all right!' Stacey said.

I lifted one from the counter. They were in pink, mint and light-apricot. I turned it around to see the price. 'Fourteen quid ninety-nine,' I told her.

She pulled a face. 'Not something I'd buy myself then. I'm forever doing that, spending all my pay in here. Defeats the purpose of working, doesn't it?' she said, like she was talking to a preschooler.

I forced a little laugh. I thought of a witty response and I even had a more thoughtful one too, like: 'It gets you out and about.' But I reasoned, why bother? Women like her don't need any encouragement. I didn't want to give her any idea that I was interested in her. Not on any level at all. Still, I wouldn't have been rude about it. I gave her a smile in response. It was enough to get her out of the road.

I lifted one of the mint-coloured books. It was pretty decent. I set it beside the till and, when all was quiet, it fell down beside my fleece coat on the floor. And when it was time for a tea break, it found itself wrapped up and subsequently in my rucksack.

It wasn't the type of thing I would buy for myself either.

I decided to start writing. I hadn't decided if I'd write fan fiction like I used to – it'd been a while – or if I'd write my thoughts. You know, cover to cover, that book ended up being about Klaudia in one form or the other. I started off writing a short story about her, began to imagine what could've happened to Maciej. Of course he didn't come up on Google. Not everything is opened out for us to read about. Some things are kept small and private and I just had to let my imagination wander. One page per story. A mix of truth and fantasy.

It was meant to stay private.

Then she got in touch. Klaudia called one day, said she'd been busy, but that she was looking for something permanent with more hours. I told her about the full-time job. At least one of us should have it, I thought.

'You should go for it,' I said.

'Are *you* not going to? Hugo said that you might.'

'Hugo? Nah . . . you apply,' I said.

'I don't know, I fancy trying to get back into teaching,' she said.

She'd been a teacher in Poland, apparently. I realised I didn't know Klaudia well at all if she hadn't even told me that.

'Oh yes, for a few years, kindergarten.'

'What age are you, Klaudia?'

'Thirty-one,' she said.

It hit me. She was older than *Stacey*, quite possibly, but yet I'd seen her as so much younger. Then the more I thought about her face, I realised her skin looked so good because she was fresh-faced, free from every scrap of make-up. She was a full decade older than me, there was no way anything could've happened between us. She had an awareness of herself, like when she was eating. I decided she was *too* self-aware and *too* hidden, too on the surface and too much under it. No, I wasn't sure if I knew Klaudia one wee bit.

I wondered what I could write about her that wouldn't seem peculiar. Da could be a nosey bastard, you know, so I wrote notes.

I've only ever written one diary in my life – if you don't count this, and I wouldn't, it's not a diary, maybe a reconciliation of sorts – but that mint embroidered book I knew I would do something with. I just had a feeling.

It was Jasmine I should've been writing about, but my mind didn't work like that. She was getting on with life and its trappings. But Klaudia was still an enigma, like Da. I wanted the people who didn't love me to do it, to just love me. Was it really so hard to do?

When I was thirteen or fourteen, a group of kids in school had it in for me. I couldn't think about the people who liked me – well, there were one or two who found me tolerable – I just thought about those other guys all the time. Would I ever make them like me? Would I want them to like me? Would I tell them to leave me be?

This replayed over and over, the forgetting all the good stuff, until I was lonely in uni knowing no one, and the bad guys from school faded – part of the way – and I realised that none of that mattered. I'd wasted so much energy thinking about the people who hated me and who I hated back, like they were eating my brain. And I couldn't let them go until I had no one and I was lying in bed at night. And then I'd dream about the couple of guys who didn't hate me.

They'd always be asking me to do something and I'd be saying: 'Yes, let's go.' I'd be grabbing my coat or checking my pockets for change but they'd be away. Gone. Because I let them go. I did. Not just in my dreams. That's the kind of stuff that went on in my head when I was alone in bed and that was one of the reasons that I liked Jasmine to be there, because then I had a whole new batch of things to be cross about, but no faces to pin them to, and so it meant that when we slept together I slept better.

Strange things happen when you lie on a bed with someone.

In bed, Jasmine would turn away from the centre, subconsciously, it seemed, stealing the sheets, winding herself like a key on the lid of a corned-beef tin. If I woke she'd be hidden in among them, and I'd be able to just doze off and not need to look under my bed

5 June

Jasmine has become a caricature of herself these days. Her eyes, in my mind, are even bigger than I know they are, and I'm sorry I never took any photos of that pretty little face to remind me.

Jasmine was the last person I was with sexually. First and last. There, now you know.

Uni put me in touch with two lads, Kyle and Farris, and together we rented a student house. Jasmine was Kyle's cousin. She visited the student house a couple of times before it happened. Kyle would ignore her, staying in his room lifting weights when she called. Farris would be hidden in his room too, in a marijuana cloud and a James Ellroy passage. There was never a danger of them answering the front door. They ignored callers completely unless preceded by some end-of-class arrangement, text message or the undeniable clinking of glass bottles inside an off-license bag in the hand of someone stood on the doorstep. It was up to me to be hospitable

I didn't know what to talk to Jas about, I told her that Kyle wasn't yet back and she asked for a drink so I fetched her a can of orange Fanta from Kyle's shelf in the fridge and we sat together for a while watching a game show. I answered a few questions to impress her, then, when I didn't know an answer, I would go out on a limb and try to conjure up some small talk.

I hadn't a baldy how to ask a question that wasn't closed, and so she just sat on the sofa chirping 'Yeah' and 'Nah,' which didn't help. The last time I'd really been with a girl, for any amount of time, I was only about eleven. So seven or so years before. Speaking to girls was a faint, ebbing memory. The girls in my uni classes were too aloof, with their flicky hair and their tight jeans. They instantly thought you wanted to ride them, like they held something over you. Even the minging ones. Like the Staceys, they had that air about them, like I probably found them irresistible. Which, believe me, I didn't.

It was October. A different October, a different year. Despite the cold Jasmine wore a turquoise top that showed her midriff, exposed her arms and the little white lines across them. Little healed cuts. Little not-quite scars.

She took a sip and then she looked at me with those big eyes, the skin on her forearms getting goose-bumped. Farris, Kyle and I never bothered with lighting fires or setting draught excluders in the doorways like people did back home in the land of the living dead.

'Can't you flick a switch?' she asked me.

'Hold on a minute,' I said. I left the room.

'Where you going, Scott?'

'To get an electric heater,' I called from the hallway, just needing to get away. 'I think there's one in . . .'

'Don't bother with that.'

When I came back into the room, reddening slightly, Jasmine had her hand out like she was waiting for her change in a shop, her eyes on my jumper, clearly wanting what she would call a 'lane' of it.

I took it off over my head, ruffling my hair, which I swiftly flattened back down into place along with my glasses, which had also gone skew-whiff. Jasmine pulled my jumper over her shirt, mussed her dark, waist-length hair out of the neckline, over her shoulders and down her back.

'We'd mebbies be warmer goin' tae bed,' she said, ducking her face into the neckline as if she was sniffing the material.

I shuffled about, self-conscious in a T-shirt that showed too much of my own arms, which were much less appealing than hers. I held them behind my back.

I looked at her shoes, neat little laces resting on black patent, like Klaudia's shoes the night at the lighthouse. Sensible brogues, clearly not designed with girls like Jasmine in mind.

'With you. I want tae go bed with you, Scott.' She stood. I looked at her, I suspect my mouth was agape or something because she laughed and said, 'Are you deaf as well as blind?'

'Not blind,' I said.

'Okay, are we doing this, or will I go? Not gettin' the hint, are you? A bit slow . . . as well as blind?'

She tapped the glass of one lens with her fingernail and smiled coyly. Jas had amber splashes circumnavigating the pupils in her chocolate-brown eyes, her nose cutely turned up at the end.

'You sure?' I asked her.

It'd been me who wasn't. Not initially.

Jasmine just sighed and went to turn towards the front door.

'No. Stay,' I shouted after her.

I just never expected it to happen like that. I thought I'd be drunk my first time, or at least be in a pub, not just sitting watching TV and my housemate's cousin calling to 'show her face', and end up propositioning me in the fusty old living room over a can of Fanta.

Those things didn't happen to *me*. But I suppose they had to happen to someone, sooner or later, and that was just the way they did.

Jasmine did an about-turn and started up the stairs, her hands held in front of her, leaving the banisters untouched as if she was floating upward, as if she was cautious not to leave a trace of herself on anything but me.

'Which room?' she asked.

'Top floor,' I said.

She climbed the next set of stairs past Kyle's room. 'That where *shit for brains* sleeps?'

'Your cousin?'

Jasmine nodded, although I soon learnt that she hated me calling Kyle her cousin. Weeks later she said: 'I don't even know the mug. My dad keeps askin', "Have you been round to see your cousin yet? He doesn't know Newcastle, make the lad feel welcome," you know . . . all that guff?'

'I know,' I'd said.

Not that I did know what it's like to have a cousin, or even if it means anything significant. But Kyle, he was settling just fine for being in a strange city. Fact was Kyle settled like the rain. He was the sort just made for uni, it was in his breeding, in every aspect, except maybe the work which maybe – or 'mebbies', as his cousin often said – didn't come too naturally for him. But the partying, boozing and bed-hopping he was good at, and being accountable to no one. That too.

At the top she looked around at two doors, one left open by me when I'd heard her knock. My room was on the right, the one with the fresh, but badly assembled Ikea furniture and the posters of *Batman* and *Kick-Ass* stuck to the walls.

'What age *are* youse?' Jasmine asked me.

'What age are *you*?' I batted back.

Jasmine gave me a look like I was wasting her time. I felt like I was when she sat on the bed looking at the saucers in the defunct fireplace, the jars of dirty melted wax, virtually no wick and still never thrown out, like Granny's soap miser she bought from the Betterware catalogue once. She'd put the slivers of fiddly soap bars into it and apply some pressure until they melted into one piece, all different colours, marbled together into quite a better-looking thing at times, depending on the originals.

'Have youse got a light?' Jasmine asked.

I nodded and took the lighter from the top sock drawer, where my spare razor blades and belts were coiled at the side of neatly rolled-up balls of socks. She shook the lighter and lit the stubs of two candles.

'The rest are dead,' Jasmine state-the-fucking-obvious said.

I joined her on the edge of the bed. She sat on top of my thighs, her toes poking the undersides of my knees. She was up close, I could see the tiny open pores on the sides of her nose, the loose eyelash that was resting on the bed of other lashes.

Jasmine took my glasses off, folded them and set them on the bedside table. She went out of focus. She smelt all sugary and acidic at the same time. I felt like I should kiss her, like it was the next step, but she wouldn't let me. She unbuttoned my jeans instead. Jasmine, in her skirt, pushed her knickers to the side.

'I'm on the pill,' she breathed in my ear as she pushed me back so I was lying down, watching her, wearing my jumper, on top of me. I tried to put my hand up the jumper but she grabbed my wrists, clamped my hands above my head. Strands of her hair tasted soapy and perfumed as they fell into my mouth. Then my every sense was flooded with her.

'Stop,' I said, putting my hands on her hips. Jasmine looked like she was going to hit me, she lay down and let me spoon her until she fell asleep.

I lay there awake, listening to her breathing change. She got heavy on my arm. Not that she was heavy, and she wasn't tall, not that I would ever go with a tall girl. Not that I'd ever have went for her. Jasmine had gone for me after all.

The first girl I met in Newcastle, my first week, the first visitor to the house and she and I had got together, and for the next two and a half years it was only her.

When I was out with Farris and Kyle I never tried it on with anyone else. They'd egg me on, especially with big fat girls. 'C'mon, Scott, give her a buck, dare ya!' they'd say, but there was no need to try with anyone, not when there was Jas.

★

The notebook sat in my hands in bed. I wondered about writing about Jasmine but I couldn't write about what I knew. I wanted to think about everything I didn't know. I wrote a poem about Klaudia that was really about Jasmine, in hindsight: a Polish girl in an oversized jumper was leading me by the hand, we met by the water, there were seagulls, she had amber in her eyes. This poem-girl was clearly an amalgamation of them both. Then I got stuck.

The last time I wrote a poem my granny wasn't even a pensioner. Back then she still dyed her hair back to its original red. Back then she walked me home from school. I tried to remember how my poem had gone, to recite it to Granny because I'd been pleased with it in school.

It was in Primary 3, Mrs Fletcher had me go to the portacabin classroom next-door to read it to Miss Ambrose, so it must've been good – or maybe she was taking the piss. Maybe it was so stupid it would be their secret joke and they'd laugh about it in the staff room, like when I was asked to write on the chalkboard what foxes' young were called, and I wrote 'cubes' instead of 'cubs' and Mrs Fletcher said: 'That sounds painful!'

I heard her tell Miss Ambrose in the playground when they came out to relieve the dinner lady – or playground supervisor, as Mrs Dudley liked to be known. The two of them had a great laugh over it. So, when I had to go and read the poem next door, I just stood at the side of the portacabin instead. I counted to sixty, one whole minute ought to have been long enough I reckoned, then I went back inside and Mrs Fletcher said, 'Well Scott, what did Miss Ambrose say about your poem?' and I said, 'She liked it.'

'But *what* did Mrs Ambrose say?' Miss Fletcher asked.

'She said, "Very good, Scott,"' I mumbled, unsure what her response would've been or if I'd said something embarrassing again that I didn't understand.

Then I went back to my seat beside Ryley, wee pocket rocket, the snotters tripping her, her bird's-nest hair. I sat beside her year in year out because I was the good child who would be a good influence on the like of her.

Now Ryley's a trainee doctor. Her. Out of everyone in that room!

And six months ago she stood beside the surgeon. Ryley looked scared shitless that she knew me. She was relieved there were officers either side of my bed. And now I'm in here, thinking about poems and girls I hardly ever knew, not really, and the one I sat beside every day for all those years, and I'm realising that I probably knew them all as much as anybody is ever going to let me, and more than anyone ever will again.

1 July

The summer started like this: Da was about the house a lot and so was I.

I never got the job, the full-time one in the Nurseries. And yes, I did apply in the end. Klaudia got it instead. Then I saw that Klaudia had wanted it all along, decided not to return to teaching.

Teachers weren't retiring – I say 'weren't' as if it was a long time ago, when really everything I'm telling you was recent enough, and if anything ever really changes in this country it's just that it's hard to picture from here.

I picture the world turning in a completely different direction outside the slow gravitational pull of this place.

So teachers stayed on. And Hugo, well he was virtually a relic by the time he rolled out of the classroom and into Perry's. At least he'd done something different with his life other than spend it in classrooms, I suppose.

It was on the news too: a whole country filled with young fresh meat – in teacher terms – and they couldn't get jobs because of the Hugos who wouldn't take pensions, or couldn't take pensions. Had become accustomed to the lifestyle. That swanky teacher salary with all its benefits. See, all politics! So Klaudia never stood a chance of getting back behind the desk.

For Hugo the Nurseries was a part-time job which had led to a full-time one. He was telling me once that his wife had left him because she wanted to retire, move to Spain and he didn't. Although you wouldn't know it to hear him go on about the place. He had it in his head that he was invaluable to Perry's. None of us were. Eventually, he decided that enough was enough and buggered off to Spain to win back 'the wife', as he called her, and Klaudia got his old supervisor job.

Her old job went too, but it wasn't posted on the notice-board, this time it was done on the quiet. Forget equal opportunities! Another 'Stacey' was drafted in, while I was given four hours, just weekends, if I was lucky.

They recruited two students: a big rugby-playing fella and a girl I recognised from the village. And they took loads of hours between the two of them.

Klaudia was in charge of rotas. She would phone me to tell me my hours. It was the most contact I'd had with her in months.

'How are you doing? Do you like your new job?' I asked her.

'It is good, Scott.' She'd pause, then say something like, 'I hope you are okay again.'

She never gave me the chance to reply. I'd say something about seeing Granny, that Clint could give me more hours . . . maybe, maybe if she could . . . Klaudia always cut me up mid-sentence, 'I have to ring around here, Scott. Glad you are feeling a bit better. You sound good.' She would ring off.

I wondered what she'd meant by 'feeling better'. I'd thought that she thought I was good. Better than okay. But it could get back on track, I thought. Now she was supervisor she couldn't avoid me.

I wasn't being paranoid, but there were times when I had to ask myself if I was reading too much into other people's actions, if I walked past people and they went quiet or lowered their voices. It's not easy, you see, there's so much they could have been saying: 'Do you know who his da is?' And, in the town, people know everything about everyone. But there was no way they could've known what the dean had been insinuating with his counselling remark.

Still these ideas crept into my head, even though I'd done nothing wrong I wondered if everybody knew everything about me: Scott McAuley, lived with his granny, da was a political prisoner back in the day, Scott was threatened by his girlfriend's da in Newcastle that he would go to the peelers if McAuley Jr ever went near Jas again.

She sent me clippings today from the papers. Off the Internet. Jasmine's interested in me again. Not that she wrote anything, just her initials, PJ, followed by a sad face. I've stuck them to the wall. On my own noticeboard. The clippings give me a bad name in here, 'offensive material, purposefully provocative'. I'm caring less every day.

People forget that if they were in the papers they would buy it. I think this is what Jasmine's doing: gathering clippings for posterity. It makes me wonder what the governor has confiscated. What things I'll never receive.

I picture the people who don't understand me, I see them reading about me and understanding me even less. I picture them giving up even trying.

I'm going to write a letter to Jas today. I'll tell her I've stopped looking under my bed. That I've realised the monsters were inside me all along.

8 July

When I was younger Da took me to see *Avatar*, it was always the cinema – somewhere he could eat, not talk. This particular time he had a straggly auburn beard but his eyes were red and when he gave me a hug (which was not like him) and slapped me on the back, I could smell no booze.

For the first time he didn't fall asleep in the flicks, but he was up and down, yo-yoing about, having to go outside to make a few calls.

'It's all kicking off,' he said, whatever *it* was. I didn't ask.

On the way home he was asking what subjects I was taking for O levels.

'All of them,' I said.

'Good, that's good. How many is *all of them?*'

He wasn't listening to me, he was listening to Elton John, began to croon away, knew all the lyrics too. Some song about saving someone's life. He was nearly wistful. Wobbly even.

'Erm, four. Four,' I said, feeling myself crimson at him for singing.

'Four?' Da scoffed. 'O levels?'

'Most are only doing three O levels.'

'Sugar bear,' he sang.

He drummed on the steering wheel as he sang then he paused the CD on the ending to the only song he seemed to like.

'Oh, that's good then,' he concluded.

Da insisted on coming into the house after driving me home and waking Granny up. She'd not been feeling well I told him, but he had to. Insisted on it.

'It's okay, Scott, she'll want to hear this.' And he went in, pounding up the staircase with a stupid grin on him like I only saw on occasion.

I heard them from the front door, where I stood, feet pointed away, toes towards the living room so I could get away quickly if I was caught.

'Ma, I've met somebody,' he was saying to her.

'Have you?' Granny's voice came, empty as ash.

'Is that all you have to say . . . *have you*?'

'What do you want me to say, Edward?' her voice grew, grew a hook on the end. 'I'm glad for you, then.'

He let out a sigh. 'I was going to say that I'd bring her down to meet you, but you obviously don't want to bother.'

'Edward, just wait till it's more serious.'

'It is *serious*, Ma. You know what?' I could hear his voice coming close to the door so I backtracked away. 'I won't bother trying to be part of your family anymore. I'll just leave you pair to it.'

'That's not what I am saying.' Granny sounded exhausted.

'Fuck it. You're a joyless bitch, you know that?'

Da hammered down the stairs and walked out past me, head bowed, chin pressed to his chest, trying to make his eyes big and innocent-looking.

'I'll not be back for a while,' he said and walked out of the door, his face all sheepish but enough of the wolf in him to slam it behind him.

Out of everybody I've hurt I'm sorry it wasn't him. If I could change anything, if had a magic lamp, that's the wish I'd rub into it. It's like how I worried about the people who never had me in their thoughts. I went along, hurting the ones I loved, or liked, or was indifferent to. But Da, he deserved to be hurt and he wasn't. Not badly enough. Maybe embarrassed, definitely lonely, but not tore up. Not nearly enough.

I sat beside Granny, catching sight of her little wicker table and her potpourri in the scallop shell, a box of peach-coloured tissues, the photo of footprints in the sand with the line from this religious poem when someone asked God why there was only one set of footprints and He said: 'It was then that I carried you.' I must've looked at that photo and read those words a thousand times. No, more. Still, I can't remember it exactly.

Granny has never been religious. It always seemed like a redundant thing, like a rabbit's foot on a key ring or something. A symbol to be cruel or self-righteous. We all follow our own religions anyway, whatever we want them to mean. The rest is pot luck.

I tried to hug her but Granny tensed – she wasn't a hugger. Neither was Da, the new girlfriend must've unleashed some affection in him he thought he'd pay forward when he'd collected me, with his pally embrace.

'I'm fine, Scott . . . used to it, son,' Granny said.

'Dad looked annoyed.'

'I've seen it all before.' Granny took a tissue and dabbed her eyes with it. 'What film did you go to see?'

'*Avatar.*'

'Oh.' She pushed a smile to her lips.

'An alien thing.'

'You like it?'

I shrugged. 'Yeah. Was brilliant.'

He ruined everything.

Granny tucked her tissue into the billowy sleeve of her nightdress. 'Your da has a girlfriend.'

'Has he?' I asked, letting on I hadn't been listening.

'It's not the first time.'

This shouldn't have been a surprise but I couldn't picture any woman who wasn't my mum going near him. I couldn't even picture Mum with him. To me she was young and sweet and he was always old and bitter. I forget that at one stage they must've been on the same track.

'Wonder if his girlfriend knows what he did,' I said.

'Must,' Granny said. 'She'll not be anybody you'd want to know.'

'How's that?'

'Do ya not remember about six years ago, he showed up with this one he was working with? A parole officer, she was, he was going to marry her . . . all this carry on.'

I shook my head.

'Then I spoke to her in the kitchen. You were away . . . where were you? Oh, in Edinburgh with school. That was it. Your da had her here one day and I lapped her up, thought she could be the making of him. Next day she was here on her own, said she was excited to meet you. She had a wee boy too, younger than you were, he was being picked up from nursery by her husband.

I said, "You mean your *ex*-husband?" thinking she'd made a mistake. "Soon," she said. Then it all came out. Been doing a line with your da behind her husband's back. She was sussing us out – me and you – before deciding if it was worth jumping ship.'

Granny stopped, a tongue of regret pressing itself against the inside of her mouth.

'I take it she didn't *jump ship*.'

'No. I chased her. Your da fell out with me then too.'

'Oh my God,' I said. I laugh at my innocence, at my piety, but I was young. *Younger*. We're all different kinds of mature at seventeen. I suppose I was naive.

'Mandy – your mum – was engaged when your da started going with her. She left the fella two months before her wedding.'

She was more considerate with her words this time, or at least the pace of the delivery. Granny's eyes were questioning me, how much she could say. I was practically a man but she still watched what she said as if I was that little boy standing at the living room curtains watching out for him.

I can't deny that a shot of excitement ran through me at the thought of my mum having a fiancé. Was Granny going to tell me this other man could've been my real da?

'He always wants what he can't have, and he can't be happy with what he has, when he gets what he wants, your da,' Granny said. She never said 'my son,' never 'Duke,' nor 'my Duke,' although she'd never call him that anyway – it was always his given name, which was Edward. I never heard her say 'my Edward'.

I should say here that Da was given Duke as a nickname, after John Wayne, on account of both of them walking as though they'd shat themselves: John Wayne's scissoring gait the result of being saddle-sore; Da's was the product of a kneecapping.

After he stormed out of Granny's house we didn't see

Sugarbear again for a full year and whatever happened to the woman he'd fallen out with his family over remains a mystery. Years later, with Granny in the fold, when he'd moved his stuff into her bedroom, I recalled him walking out of that room after orchestrating the whole to-do. How easy it was for him to put his head on her pillow and sleep, just like a baby.

28 July

When my mum was growing up she had a friend called Deena. Mum and Deena were thick as thieves, grew up streets apart. My mum stayed on there when her own mum died and Uncle Ned left for England.

Up until a few weeks ago all I knew was that Deena would send me a present to Granny's when I was little and, like all contact with anybody I've ever had, it fizzled.

It was only when I was talking to someone here, where I've been moved to, in Glen House – this fella, moved too, across from Bush House. Of course I won't name him here. But he said, this fella: 'I know Deena Roberts, can tell you which street she lives on.' So I decided to write. Chanced it, no house number, no postcode. This screw just looked at it and said: 'Good luck with that.'

But Belfast is like the town. All these places are the same. Everybody knows everybody. You could get a letter in the post, the completely wrong postcode and address but the postal worker will know who you are and you'll get it regardless, and if he or she doesn't know you, someone will. That's how these things work.

When I sent Deena the first letter I wasn't expecting to hear anything back but then her letter came back within the week. My fingers trembled at the sight of new handwriting I didn't recognise. That's when I found out that my mum had lived with Deena for a time, until my da came along; she mentioned the old boyfriend too, the one Mum was engaged to briefly.

At the time Mum died Deena was living in England, like Ned, everyone wanting to escape that place at that time. Granny too, that lesser distance to the town. Sometimes I'm surprised there is anyone left in Belfast at all.

Deena said that she still thought about Mum every day, that they 'were like sisters' and that she only learnt to drive two years ago or she'd have loved to come to the town to see me, but it wasn't like the train would stop anywhere near. Deena apologised, said she should've made more of an effort. Said she was sorry I'd taken the wrong path.

Deena vaguely remembers Granny but she remembers my grandda better. She mentioned his full head of hair, which he blackened with boot polish. It killed him when my da did what he did, Deena wrote. 'Your grandfather was a gentleman.'

I know the story already: Grandda Bob McAuley had a heart fart and died. The end.

Deena often sees when Da does talks near her home, but they never really got on. 'But even though Duke doesn't visit you, you say, it's not my place to comment – at least he did the right thing in the end.'

She has every faith I'll get released early: 'Keep your head down and do as they say and I'll see you on the other side.' Deena has two sons and she'd like to think she would never give up on them. What I did was senseless, but who were the victims really, she wrote.

I wrote back straight away, asked Deena to visit. Now she's driving maybe she'll make it out to see me.

And now I wait.

2 August

When I first came home I hardly recognised the place. It was pretty much emptied out. Da had kitted Granny out for the fold the way I'd been kitted out for uni. Took it upon himself to get rid of some of the old furniture. He relocated loads to ex-prisoners freshly released. Would make us do without to carry through a promise to one of his fellas.

The kitchen table had gone and, instead, Da had made the trip to his favourite Swedish flat-pack furniture outlet and bought a corner desk he called his 'bureau'. Made a little office for himself at the end of the kitchen. He had a photo of his own da on there, Boot-Polish Bob, the gentleman who, unlike my mum, I have precisely zilch memory of. Precisely like my mum, Grandda Bob was rarely ever mentioned. Duke had a few pics of himself at podiums or shaking hands with different political leaders.

Then there were the leftovers the lodgers hadn't bothered taking with them, like bed sheets, chipped cups that came free from the filling station with a couple of tokens, baking utensils Da had strung around like ornaments.

His desk was another ornament. He sat pretending to work. It's where he made phone calls, where he perched doing phony paperwork. But I'm a nosey bastard too, in case you hadn't already guessed.

One morning last August I was standing, eating a banana, toasting bread as Da sat chain-smoking at 'the bureau'. I watched him rummage about, check his watch: a huge gold Tag Heuer jobby. He stood, went upstairs and came back down reeking of Joop.

'I've a meeting,' he said.

Who did he think he was kidding? When he left I watched

out of the window, standing back so he couldn't see. After he drove off I went to his desk and had a look about. The toast popped like corn out of hot oil. Scared the shite out of me. I checked the front window again. Da was definitely away. I knew he was hiding something.

I opened his drawers. They were full of bank statements and credit-card statements. At that stage I didn't bother with them. I found letters, invites to different events, all dated for ages ago, even years ago, and he'd brought them with him to Granny's – he was a hoarder, that was for sure. A full L-shaped desk to hold his outdated rubbish.

Then I found them, the letters that were dated the last couple of months, 'suspended pending investigation', they said, 'inappropriate advances'. There was nothing specific but I couldn't leave it at that. I memorised exactly where he'd had everything. I sliced piles in half and went through the letters, re-piled them before setting them back into the side cupboard.

There was this notebook in his teeny-tiny writing. His short-hand. I took it out and read it. It was a draft of a letter to his boss.

Dear Dave,

    In light of the allagations about me I just want to put my side of events forward, can I say firstly and fourmost that when I meet Conor's mother Jenny outside of my visits, it was just to make sure that she was coping after her son's death, the second time I didn't call in on her, I was out in a bar and it was just a chance meeting. I didn't know she worked there and if she did tell me I definately don't remember. We were two consenting adults, regardless of if she is married it is her progative who she goes to bed with. I do not believe that she was vulernable. As you

well know, I don't drink, so my jugement was as good as
it has ever been.

I had to laugh at that bit, since when was his judgement anything but ropey?

I would overlook it if her husband complained but as far
as I know he doesn't know about this, and I know that
their relationship is strained. I am not going to go into
detail about what happened between Jenny and myself
but I want to say that I will appeal this. That we met as
two consenting adults, she asked me to wait for her after
her shift. I am not in the position of power you are making out. I keep my personal and private lives seperate.

He was almighty when it suited, then meek and mild and non-
influential when he needed to crawl out of a hole.

So he'd went sniffing around, couldn't leave people alone. I
put the cover back over the notepad. There were more drafts of
it, scribbled over, but I didn't want to know any more excuses, I
was too embarrassed.

Before I put the book back I saw a box in the back of the cabinet. Inside it was a bag of white powder. I opened it. Had a look.
Cocaine. So much for being clean and sober and the talk he'd
given about addiction at Conor's funeral like he was levitating
over the mortals, probably high as a spacecake that day and all!

I took a sniff and went upstairs to lie on my bed. I watched
The Matrix, all three films back to back. Clint texted to offer
me some last-minute work but I had to decline on account of
health and safety. I took my own notepad out of my drawer and
I wrote. Alone. No one to vouch for where I was.

For the first time I didn't write about Klaudia, but about Jasmine. Jasmine and me. I wrote that I was Neo and she was Trinity, that when I touched her she turned into golden code and floated above my bed. I'd brought her with me. Jasmine. I managed to fill two pages about it. After, I was buzzing. I got into the shower. The whole day had almost managed to pass down a plughole of time.

There was a knock on the door. At first I thought I'd only imagined I'd heard the rat-a-tat-tat, until it woke me from my daze.

'Scott,' came Da's voice.

I turned off the shower and stood in the cold, feeling it settle on each bead of water that paused to listen too, before running down my body.

'We're heading out for something to eat,' he said. 'You're coming too.'

'Okay,' I peeped.

I passed his bedroom door. My da was fast expanding, it was more obvious with his shirt off. There he was, belly like a woman six months pregnant, heart tattooed on his heart, 'Mandy' – my mum's name – under it in Ye Olde English font, like she was destined to always be inked into that part of history, under his skin and degraded by the needle.

What my mum, or any girlfriend of his, ever saw in Da was beyond me. Now Conor's mum, by the sounds of things, had more sense. I felt like laughing at him, standing there, face all serious, giving out his orders.

'Hurry yourself up and get ready, Scott. Your granny wants to go out for dinner.'

'Oh,' I said, leaning against the wall, gripping the door frame. 'What's the haps?'

'Married fifty years ago today,' he spoke from one side of his mouth. There was a cotton bud hanging from the other side, which he took out and hoked about his ear with impatience and a grimace.

'Fifty years?'

'Well I'm nearly fifty.' Da binned the cotton bud and concentrated on tying his tie, straightening his collar out, folding it. 'Couple of years to go.'

I was smiling at him.

'What's that stupid grin about?' he asked me.

'What?' I giggled like a little girl.

'Hmm . . .' He looked me up and down. 'You'll need to get a move on.'

'I will. In a wee minute.'

He took a tube of gel from the top of the bedside cabinet where that footprints photo used to sit. The scallop shell was still there, full of butts and ash. The walls though, he'd painted a shade of fagnolia. He looked at himself in the full-length slid-erobes.

'I never celebrate my anniversary . . . to Mandy. Probably can't even remember it, the fourth or fifth of December. Fifth, fifth,' he said.

'Christmas wedding,' I said, it was the most time I'd spent willingly in his company in months and I had to be off my face to do it.

'Aye, Christmas wedding. Full of mixed nuts. Actually, it was just a handful of us, Gretna Green. Shotgun wedding, cause of you.' He ruffled the gel through his hair, dimming its shade to cast-iron. 'Do *you* think your granny should be celebrating when the man's been dead twenty years, or am I alone in thinking that she's flipped her lid?'

'I don't know. Yes. I suppose so. It's a big one. Pity he isn't here to celebrate with her.'

Da sighed. 'Sometimes family is no closer than strangers and sometimes strangers become your family.'

'That right?' I asked.

'That's right,' he said. He looked at me in the mirror and pulled the gel residue off his fingers with a hand towel.

'Right, I'll go and get ready.'

I walked into my room and let my towel fall to the floor. I stood bollock-naked, pulled my cream linen trousers on and a striped shirt. My feet wanted to step into the green DM boots but I caught them just before they did.

'No,' I said. 'School shoes tonight.'

I meant to say 'sensible shoes', that's just how it came out. Not warm enough for sandals.

'Talking to yourself again, head-the-ball?' Da shouted in. The walls were like paper, every strain of him on the loo was a treat upstairs too, or even from the front door.

I swapped my hoop earring for a diamond stud. Granny seemed to like it, she certainly always said plenty about it. Da hated it. Maybe that's why I chose it. I met him in the kitchen, my toast cold in the toaster from the morning, the banana skin still lying on the counter. I looked at the desk, paranoid that when I'd found the coke I'd left everything else. Of course I hadn't been so stupid, but that stupidity was coming sure as the autumn.

'What in God's name?' Da nearly wet himself on the tiles. 'Linens?'

'It's summer.'

'By the skin of its teeth. It's cool out there. You're not in Barbados, Dolly.'

Da saw my earring and had to bite his lip from saying any-thing further. I followed him out to the car. He was laughing but I knew he wasn't happy. What did he have to be happy about?

'I don't celebrate my anniversary since Mandy died,' Da repeated in the car as we pulled up outside the fold.

'Maybe Granny's lonely,' I said, looking out at her little win-dow with the curtains lined up asymmetrically.

'She *is alone*, what does she expect? We're born alone, we die alone,' he muttered and then nudged me. 'Go get Isla-Man.'

I jumped out of the car. I heard the car ticking over, purring until it began to rev. He was edging away, laughing as he did it. I looked forward then back. There he was, another bit away.

'Child,' I said to myself.

I ignored him; they say to do that to attention-seeking chil-dren, don't they? That they'll stop if they don't get the attention.

'Hello, Scott,' the nurse said, the nice nurse who Da could never get a rise out of, the one who got sweeter the ruder he was to her. 'She's waiting for you.'

I darted up the flight of stairs. There was Granny sitting, her woollen winter coat on, clutching her bag. She held my arm as I helped her down the stairs.

'Think they'd give you a room downstairs,' I said.

'No, no, others need it more than me.'

'Enjoy your anniversary evening, Mrs McAuley,' Nice Nurse shouted over.

'She's lovely, that one,' Granny said, barely out of earshot.

Nice gave me a smile which I returned.

Outside Da was back in his spot, puffing away on a feg. He shouted out of the window,

'Fucking hell, she's for the Arctic and he's for the Bahamas.' His big guttural laugh took the breath from him.

'We didn't get the shirt-and-trousers memo, sorry,' I muttered.

'What's he shouting about now?' Granny tutted, not wanting an answer. I helped her into the back of the car. 'I'm fine, Scott, love,' she said.

'Ready for a big slap-up meal?' Da said when I was in the passenger seat again.

He drove us to the village, where Da had a table reserved in the restaurant. Just outside the car park someone slowed down to let him into the spot, a man with a flat cap and a greying beard, a finger hooked to wave Da on.

'Go on,' the man mouthed. He was about seventy or so.

Da sighed. 'For fuck sake, just go,' he said, but he stayed smiling, nodding and flashing his lights to thank the man. 'If he'd just shifted I'd have got in quicker, he's blocking half the row.'

'Some people do bad by doing good,' I said.

Da swooped into the space. Granny reached in and patted me on the shoulder.

'Are we landed?' she asked.

'We're landed, Granny,' I told her.

I looked out at the inches of sea past the walls of brick, the birds going the direction of the water's pull. Gulls were landing on the church spire and the roofs of the houses closest to the front.

We got out. I stretched my legs while Da helped Granny out of her side of the car, starting to fawn. Now was his time to take over, for the benefit of the diners. Manners were wasted on nurses, did no harm to let them know they wouldn't mess Duke McAuley's mother about.

We went in the restaurant and had to wait a while to be seated. When we got to our table Granny squeezed the minibaguettes in the bread basket in the centre of the table. Tapped them with her knuckles.

'Fresh,' she said.

It was worse than Christmas. I wanted her to be able to eat with us so bad. Da looked around, laughed to himself.

'What is it?' Granny asked him, defuzzing her coat with her fingertips.

'It's like God's waiting room in here.' He tittered, taking off his own jacket and draping it over the back of his seat.

It *was* like fifty shades of grey hair, to be truthful. Not that I laughed.

The waitress came over to us, poising a pad in her left hand, a pen in her right and pushing her half-dead smile to her eyes with the edges of her mouth.

'How are you tonight? Hey, you're making a regular thing of this,' she said to Da.

For the first time in my life I think he changed colour without the help of his temper or too many rays on the sunloungers of Salou.

Granny rolled her eyes at me. I wondered if Da was giving the waitress one. Did she look desperate enough? Maybe she did. It was getting harder to know. She was in her forties, worse than a Stacey, had an ass that looked flat as if a drinks tray was up the back of her skirt. I could just picture him in there one night, snorting his coke off the toilet cistern, getting the horn. Sorry, it'd make you sick, not that anybody wants to hear about my sexploits with Jasmine but the saying 'there's someone for everyone' just can't include him. Just can't.

The waitress came back with our menus. She handed one to Granny, who recoiled. It made me have to slow-breathe bad thoughts to the backseat of my mind to keep calm. I was coming down something anxious and awful.

'Well, I don't need to look at this. I'm having the steak,

chips, tobacco onion rings,' Da said.

'I haven't had a steak in . . .' Granny smiled. 'You know what, love? I'll have a steak too,' she said passing her menu to Flat Arse. Da's face was a picture.

'Do you do veggie sausages?' I asked.

'No, but there's loads of vegetarian options.'

The waitress ran her finger down the section of the menu Granny had just handed back. I didn't want to hold the proceedings back by looking. I was starving.

'Lasagne?'

'We do vegetarian lasagne,' she grinned. 'With chips?'

'Salad please,' I said.

'Great, I'll get Stephen to take your drinks order.' She paused like she was thinking on something. 'Did you hear the news?'

'The only news we know is that it's my ma's golden wedding anniversary,' Da said.

'Aww, congratulations.' She thumped her pen against her little square pad, menus tucked under one bingo wing. 'But no, it's . . . on the other side of the village it's all cordoned off, did you not see the police?'

Da was suddenly serious, straightening up in his seat.

'A man was found dead in his garage.'

Flat-Arse gave the look expected of people breaking news of death, a look learnt from *CSI Miami* or *Midsomer Murders*.

'Suicide?' Granny asked.

'No,' Da said, 'must be suspicious circumstances.' The voice of authority.

'Who was it?' I asked the waitress. I knew a few people in the village, is why I asked. A few ones in Perry's lived there.

She lowered her head and voice. 'Bertie Beattie. He was a regular in here. It's awful.'

'Good God!' Granny said.

'You know him, Granny?' I asked.

'No.'

'Oh.'

This took Da's mind off Granny's ordering the steak. Until it came and he remembered his puzzled face, which he didn't bother to hide as he went back to wondering why Granny had ordered a steak when she couldn't eat anything.

'Looks lovely, doesn't it?' Granny said.

She unfolded her napkin from the table and set it onto her lap, Da watched her, his fork pinning his steak down like it was going to get up and walk away, the juices coming out of it, swimming his plate, sogging his chips.

Granny cut a bit off, put a small triangle in her mouth. I started to worry about dementia, that she had forgot she had a tube up her nose going into her stomach, that she really was going to eat the thing, that it would get stuck or she would be ill and because Da had done a palm-off job he didn't know the first thing to do in that scenario. And I hadn't been given the opportunity to learn. I didn't want to startle her, or patronise.

I looked at Da, still sitting with his fork in his steak like something comical-looking. He hadn't even lifted his knife yet, he was staring at her with his little pinprick pupils.

Granny, with a slice of steak in her mouth, was moving it all around. Chewing, chewing. She had this little look on her face I don't think I've ever seen. Contentment. That was what it was. She was so absolutely fucking delighted.

'Ma.' Da had to spoil it. Because that's what he does. 'Don't you be swallowing that!' he said.

She lifted her napkin to her mouth and spat it out. 'Just wanted the taste,' she said.

Da was shaking his head, jaw hanging open.

'Da,' I said to him as Granny twisted the napkin into a little parcel and set it beside her plate. 'I'm just nipping to the loo.'

'Okay, Dolly,' Da chirped. 'A pish or a shite?'

I saw Granny put her fork down again and him, him getting tore in. I walked out into the foyer and into the toilet. When I was in a cubicle I just sat. I could hear the old lad at the sink talking to another man who'd just come out of the other cubicle next to mine.

'Did you hear about Bertie?' he was saying in this posh accent that sounded familiar, like he was off the telly.

'Bertie?'

'Ah, Bertie Beattie. Murdered today, he was.'

'Who's he?' came the other voice. 'An actor, like?'

'No, sir. Bertie is from the village, near the carriageway end.'

'Oh, sorry, I'm not a local,' the man told the posh old boy.

He sighed, the old boy. His disappointment slid round the sides of the toilet door and landed on me.

'Well, what happened to him, like?' asked the man, voice number two.

'Killed in his garage, I don't have all the details yet. Here, sir,' then there was a big, almighty pause. I sat squinting, waiting, wondering what was going on, then the old boy spoke again, 'Which, erm . . . direction did you come in from?'

'The city.'

'All right. Enjoy your dinner, sir.'

'Right,' the man said.

The door swung open and I heard one leave, water being run, the hand-dryer blasting and then the other one left too. I got up and went out, leant over the sinks and looked at my eyes. They were fine, my pupils. Big but not massive. I washed my hands even though I hadn't went to the toilet. There is stuff on toilet doors you wouldn't want on your hands or in your food. I stood at the hand dryer, the noise of it reverberating around my head.

In the restaurant Old Boy was talking to people waiting for a table, telling them the news about Bertie. I passed the waitress. Bad for business, he is, I felt like saying, but it sounded like something that would come out of my da's mouth so I caught it, killed it, binned it.

I saw Granny looking all around her. There was a stack of napkins on the service table, I must've lifted twenty. I went over and set them beside her without a word. Da wasn't impressed of course, but she looked at them and then she sliced herself another piece of steak. Da was nearly done his already. I got stuck into my own dinner, been in the toilet longer than I'd meant to and my lasagne was freezing.

'Youse hear the news? Bertie Beattie's just been found dead in his garage,' came that voice again. Over my shoulder Old Boy was standing, white linen trousers, a tweed coat, pork-pie hat. White hair down to his shoulders. Worked his way up to us already.

'Ach, Larry,' Granny said. 'Isn't that absolutely awful.' She removed her steak from her mouth and gift-wrapped it.

'God, aye, Bertie was just in here the other . . . erm.'

Larry snapped his finger and thumb like he might break into a barbershop quartet, like we three would stand, shove our chairs back and join in, snapping our fingers, swaying our heads, singing, 'Bertie Beattie, won't you please come home.'

'Sorry, aye, he was in here the other . . . whatchamacallit?' Larry said.

Da looked at me and almost laughed.

'The other *night*?' I asked Larry.

'Yes. Night. A nice man, Bertie. The locals will be devastated.' Larry's voice was clipped, his eyes watery, you could nearly see a public school boy under the old ragged blow-in he'd become.

'Here,' came Duke, the voice of authority, 'these things bring out a sense of community, wait till you see. The village will be strengthened by people's charity.'

'Silver linings.' I winked at Da.

'So it wasn't car fumes?' Granny asked.

'No. Stabbed, Isla. You know how word gets round,' Larry said.

'That's dreadful. I don't recognise the name,' Da said, as if he was trying to work out if Bertie was 'connected'. Da was shaking his head like he was sickened, him sawing the fat off his steak – he'd eat that too, left till last.

I thought about the alleyway and the two Catholic teens and the blade in Da's hand. Sometimes I can't help it. It's hard to picture, but it happened. I don't think we should forget that it did. Nobody's gonna forget my faux pas in a hurry, now are they?

But that night I looked at Da and wondered how exactly he did it. What feelings went through him at the time and if he liked that feeling of the blade going in. If he ever felt like doing it again.

'It's enough to make you sick,' said Larry.

'It's rightly put you off your dinner, I see,' Da said.

Larry turned to look at Da, I noticed how his jacket was bunched over rounded shoulders and splayed out frill-like at the back of him. 'Oh, no, I'm a pensioner. I don't pay these prices, I had my supper at home.'

Da screwed his face up at me as if to say, What's he doing in a restaurant then?

'Well, thought I'd come anyway, let people know I'm . . .' then came another big pause.

I carried on eating and so did Granny, I hoped she wouldn't forget herself and get caught up in the chewing of things. The reflexes.

'Sorry,' Larry said.

'Larry has Parkinson's disease, don't you, love?' Granny said.

'What's that?' Da asked him. 'Is that when you can't stop interviewing people?'

Larry howled with laughter. 'Man dear, you are a terrible case!'

'Laughter's the best medicine,' Da told me.

'You any interviews coming up, Da?' I asked, thinking of his appeal date. His letter to his boss.

'What?' he asked, but distractedly because Larry was telling us that Bertie used to belong to the bowling club he went to.

No harm to him but I was sick of listening about Bertie-fucking-Beattie. If that makes me sound callous then I'm sorry, I'm callous.

'It's my Granny's anniversary, her golden one,' I said.

'Aye, you know what else is golden?' Da asked Larry. 'Silence.' He put his index finger to his lips.

'You are on form this night,' Larry said, strangely loving Da's banter. 'You still in the town, Isla?'

Granny nodded into her napkin.

'Give us a shout when you're heading home.' Larry left for the next table, to spread the news. *Roll up, roll up, Bertie Beattie's taken one in the gut.* Or wherever he took one.

I *think* the conversation went in that order. See, trying to remember it back – especially when I'm getting one of my dizzies – it jumbles things up. It still annoys me, the things Da was saying to Larry.

By the end of the meal there were twenty twisted napkins on Granny's plate. Da ordered a sweet and an Irish coffee and of course a sweet wouldn't have worked for Granny, little bits would've gone down the wrong way so she declined, even when I was spurring her on.

Flat Arse came and took the plates away, brought me my green tea.

'Weak as water,' Da said when he saw how I took the teabag out straight away.

'Sure, I used to like warm water on its own. With a slice of lemon it's very good for you. For your digestion,' Granny said.

'Bad for your teeth though,' I said.

'Is that right?' she asked.

'Yeah, very acidic.'

'Enjoy that, Ma?' Da asked, not in a nice way.

'I did, Edward, thanks. But I'm paying for this.' Too sharp for him.

'Are not indeed!'

'I am. It was my idea.'

'I'm not having you pay for your own anniversary meal that you can't even eat, though you did a good job of sucking all the juice out of it.'

How I stopped myself from saying 'No Da, you did!' will never cease to amaze me.

'I'll pay,' I offered. I had a wallet full of cash from a job with Clint.

'Dolly, you save your pennies for your boot sales,' Da said, he stood up and went over to the waitress. Granny lost her sheen.

'How d'you know Larry?' I asked to take her mind off her son being a hateful cretin, least until he got back to the table.

'Larry's just one of those folk everybody knows.'

I nodded. Larry was a few tables away. He saw Da at the bar, settling the bill, shoving a handful of mint imperials into his trouser pocket, giving the look of some fungal growth sprouting beside his ball sack. Larry appeared behind him when we stood to leave, and he followed us to the front door.

'Who has a camera?' Larry asked.

'Nobody,' Da said, abruptly.

'I do, on my phone,' I corrected.

'C'mon, I have to get a photo of this lovely family, on such a special umm . . .'

'Special day,' Granny slotted in.

'What? The day Bertie Beattie snuffed it?' Da's face feigned sincerity.

I glowered at him, took my phone from my pocket and gave it to Old Boy Larry. Granny stood, holding onto Da's arm while he put his arm over my shoulder, like my shoulder was inanimate, like mock wooden stocks from an old Blackpool photo from his childhood.

Larry took the snap, his hands trembled.

'Take it again, just in case,' I said. 'Just keep taking them.'

We had to get out of the way of the influx of diners a few times. I'd never seen the restaurant so busy.

'The bad news is bringing everybody out,' Da said, and he was right for once.

I thanked Larry and took my phone back. We tried to shake him but he followed us to the car park. As we were getting in the car he lingered.

'You heading back to the town, Isla?' he asked.

'Yes,' I answered.

'Get on in,' Granny said, though Larry already had the door opened for himself.

'I just live on the way. At the point,' he said.

'You walk here?' Da asked, looking deflated, humpy head back on.

Granny and Larry were in the back, Da and myself up front.

'My neighbour gave me a lift, she's over at the bar.' Larry pointed at the pub on the waterside. 'Carole's out for the night, she's gonna get a taxi home.'

'No, that's a waste of cash,' Da said. 'Scott, you should drive Carole's car for her. Go on, she's maybe left the keys in the ignition, jump in and take Larry home.'

My elbow itched to dig him one in the side of his stupid head. Bang, bang, bang.

'Sure Scott can't drive,' Granny told him.

The innocence of Granny and Larry's faces as they smiled. 'I know! I'm just keeping him going,' said Da.

Larry patted Da's arm, chuckling away when he didn't know what in the hell he was laughing at, nor the malice behind it, and I was stuck, unable to say anything back. It'd be like me handing Da his steak knife and saying at the dinner table, 'Go on Da, stab those boys at the next table, go on, stab them the fuck to death. Nah! Just keeping you going, Da!'

But he could get away with saying whatever he wanted.

I saw Larry in the wing mirror and realised I knew him. When I was younger he used to make a habit of calling in on Granny for a coffee. Then he missed his bus to the point a few times and stayed for dinner.

It became a bit of a regular occurrence and soon Larry expected to call every Monday. Yes, I think it was a Monday thing. It was company for them both. He probably did the same thing all around the town. Had a different woman cook for him every day of the week.

'No skin on Larry's face,' Phyllice said one day, 'he's shameless.' Phyllice was Granny's friend from next door; when she died Callum and Aoife took the house on.

Then Da called in, which was unlike him. He was a Sunday-night kind of guy, nursing a hangover and the bud of a promise to be a better dad the next week. I remembered him seeing Larry at the table in the kitchen with Granny and me, and him getting his humpy head on then too, telling Granny, once she'd shooed Larry on, that everyone would think they were 'carrying on'.

They weren't. But what if they were? She would barely have been mid-fifties, if even. I'm sure plenty of people are still 'at it' by that age. But the way Da said 'everyone' would be talking about her is what did it. Ended it.

She tutted at Da, twisted her mouth at him, but she listened to him, the fool, she listened to him too. Deep down she thought what he was saying was right.

When we were all in a car together, Granny was remembering too. Larry probably only very vaguely recalled her dinners, and Da had no idea who the man even was.

15 August

Granny was led to believe I'd earned my degree. She didn't know the ins and outs of the academic year. Just presumed I'd finished early. When I thought she wouldn't question anything about it, she went and threw a spanner in the works, said the granddaughter of some woman from her fold was graduating. So then I had to weave into my web that I was graduating too.

I stayed away for a few days, pretended I was in England. And no, I didn't get all cunning and Photoshop a fake graduation pic or anything like that. Instead I created a diversion. I took my phone, printed off the image from our meal in the village – the only one that was clear, not blurred by Larry's shakes. Granny took it, said that she'd have to get a frame for it. She had this other frame. 'A nice brass one I'm keeping for your graduation photo,' is what she said. I told her I'd go ahead and slot the photo Larry took of us into the brass one for her.

'Sure I'll get you another nice frame when the university photographers *finally* get round to posting mine. No one, not Kyle, nor Farris, nor any of my uni friends, have received theirs yet,' I said, to add some authenticity. Hoping she'd forget completely.

'Hope they weren't cowboys, these photographers,' she said.

No, just your grandson is one of those, I didn't say.

Weeks later I was walking home from visiting her, cutting through the graveyard when I looked at my phone again, checking for absent texts, skimming my photos, when I found that one of us the anniversary night. It repulsed me. Da's face between mine and Granny's. I deleted it. Deleted all that I had of him, and there weren't many.

That's how, when the media used that photo in the papers, I knew it came from her. Granny'd been cut off the side, just me and Da were exposed. He's brimming with golden-anniversary festiveness. I'm serious-looking. I think I was mid-word, telling Larry to press the button again. Gives me the look the papers must've loved: red-eyed, face gaunt, though nowhere near as drawn as it is now.

The thought of one of the nurses stealing the photo, or a journalist making their way into the fold, pretending to look for a place for a fictional, aging parent, snooping around. Or worse – the unimaginable – Granny selling me out, saying: 'Here, take this, I'm done with them both.' Well, that's the worst case. And her special meal, or the memory of it, being destroyed in the process.

You, I know, would rather be nameless than have a bad name, but I personally don't care. It's more the thought of Granny being involved. It's not that I'm averse to having my photo on the front pages.

20 August

'What's wrong with your gurny bake, like?' Da said when I let the door slam. The door chain swinging. Up and down. Knock-knock.

'What's wrong with me?' I was yelling like I'd never yelled at him before – or since, come to think.

'Yes. What's wrong with you? You nearly took that front door of its bracket.'

'Take a look at yourself, would you ever?' I was squealing.

Really squealing. I couldn't control the way I sounded. I surprised myself the most by it, I think. It was just him, him rubbing me up the wrong way: looks, the things he said. Always negative. Always cutting.

'The things you were saying to Larry . . . who do you think you are?'

Da said, 'Who? Michael Parkinson? He deserves a good boot in the balls!'

'You were looking at your own mother like you were disgusted by her for something she can't help. She had cancer.'

'Oh, *I know* cancer,' Da said. 'You were the one that was away, swanning around England, pretending to do something *fancy* with your life. Ending up squirting it up the wall.'

I remember word for word. I remember thinking it could've

been himself he was talking about. They say always tell the truth and you'll never need to recall what your side of the story was. And I abided by that. I did. In here though, there are a different set of rules. Truth means nothing in here. You must find that yourself.

Anyway, my heart was thudding so much it felt like it was the only thing I could properly pay any attention to. So maybe, if there is a slight 'give' in my version, that'll be the reason why. But I'm doing my best with what I have left.

'I don't mind my ma wanting a taste of a thing, but to pick the dearest thing on the menu,' he was saying.

Unlike Granny calling him 'your da' when she spoke to me about him, relocating the ownership of Duke McAuley onto me, he thought everything was his. A hand on every rung of the ladder.

The only exception to this was my mum. She was simply 'Mandy'. Never 'your mum', nor 'my Mandy'. No, he'd be fooling no one with that pretence.

He never cared about my mum. She was just a conquest he had to mention a couple of times a year to make me think that he gave a shit.

Everything was Da's, you know: I have to help 'my fellas'. This is 'my son' home from university. *Tally ho, old chap!*

Back from doing 'fancy' things. So 'fancy', those student digs.

Even the things he didn't want were his. Conor's mum was no longer Conor's mum to me, he'd cocked his leg, marked her too. Every goddamn thing belonged to Duke McAuley. Probably had his claws in you too.

I'd nearly forgot that my anger had started with his looks at Granny in the restaurant. I was just seeing him sleeping in cinemas, leaving me standing at the window, waiting for him to come and get me, letting me down again. That's exactly where he was standing then, at that same window.

Da was mid-curtain-pull. My fists and jaw clamped.

'It was *her* dinner,' I said, sounding calmer now, my heart still pumping its music around my head.

I rubbed my temples as discretely as I could, but it was the start of me shrugging off the discrete, you know? If I had to pinpoint things, I'd say it was that day, the golden anniversary. That was the turning point.

'Listen to yourself, son. You're having a nervous breakdown or something.' *Bluster, bluster.*

'No, you listen to me . . .' I swayed, rolled on the balls of my feet. 'My granny offered to pay.'

I said *my* granny, to cut him. She was mine. She hated him.

'She doesn't have the means,' Duke spat. 'Choice comes with having the means.'

'I would've paid.'

'You *will pay*, boy,' he said. 'Don't think for one minute I don't want back what you owe me for university fees and furniture, for student accommodation . . . do you want me to go on?'

'I'm owed it!' My head on the cusp of exploding. 'You never put your hand in your pocket once for the first eighteen years of my life.'

I walked out the door and ran up the stairs, the words 'my life', 'my life', 'my life' pumped inside my blood vessels.

It *was* my life. I didn't have to answer to him anymore. I could just hear him laughing. That was his response to everything – that bitter, stuck-for-words laugh – but it didn't work on me. *Gotcha!*

I suppose I should think myself lucky that he has given up on me. Who wants to listen to all that hatred? I picture him, in the visiting room, with one of his new projects. The one-sided conversation. Promises he would carry through for some people. Deedee with her bookcase. His fellas. Getting them sorted with accommodation. All that carry on.

But me, who wouldn't have been here, there or anywhere if it wasn't for his recklessness, his impregnating seventeen-year-old Mandy. Me, who kept my head down. Worked. Never got into trouble. It was me Da hated. Hated me for holding him back, for not being a 'Belfast boy', for looking like my dead mother, for being the good son to Granny that he never was. The list goes on. It goes on.

Duke's footsteps never came along the hall. He left. Soon all I could hear was knocking coming from Callum's side of the wall between our two homes. We'd woken his kids. Or maybe it was one of the kids bashing a toy against the wall, I thought, at the time.

I got into bed in my linens and I put my fingers in my ears. That's the only upshot of a huge argument and all that emotion, I sleep well after, don't need to go online or watch a movie to get me over or even pop a pill. I slept like a rock.

The next day it was as though it had never happened.

'Right, Scott?' Duke said.

He was at his bureau, farting about on his mobile phone. So he'd gone out for a drive or something. I hadn't heard him return. I took a slice from the loaf in the freezer, dropped it into the toaster. Ate a banana. Groundhog Day.

'Those wee bastards next door were making a right noise this morning,' he said.

'Were they?' I hadn't heard a thing except the bones squeaking inside my index fingers.

'You must sleep like the dead. They were banging the bin lid up and down at six this morning, the kids have been running about through our yard since seven,' Duke said, not turning away from what it was he was so engrossed in.

It was 'our yard' then, when he wanted me on side.

'They used to always run through the yard when Granny was here.'

I was instantly sorry I said it.

Duke wrote on an envelope, he put a letter into it. Probably his letter about Conor's mum. What I'd have given to read what he thought was an appropriate response to his boss in the end. What I'd have given to know what he did to the poor woman.

'See these wee bastards today?' Duke said. 'They all know their rights. You can't say anything to them. When I was young, if I was messin' the neighbours about, my da would've expected that they hit me a clout, then he'd have gave me a clout for getting the first clout. Then all this banning the cane in schools came in. That's why kids are the way they are.'

This makes him sound like he would've hit me. Truthfully, he never lifted a finger to me, well, not until then. If he had a son he'd been there for, maybe he would've given him a good slap for misbehaving. With his history it's what I would've expected.

It was all right for his fellas, even if they thought he was a knob, they would soon see the back of him, especially if he was only one of a few different visitors. They probably thought he was all right and, don't get me wrong, I used to have an idea that he was. I believed in his all-right-ness. No, more than that. I was brainwashed to love him. *My da* was sick in hospital for a few years and it was better to keep away. Better to love him from a distance.

When he was no longer being entertained at Her Majesty's pleasure, Duke McAuley needed space to get his strength up. I thought he was going to come and take me to Belfast to live. Belfast, with its newsagents and the park with the climbing frame, Mrs Wright, maybe even Deena, but I can't remember if I had any memories of her.

It seemed that when he'd get 'out of hospital' my life would change, but we all know the truth of the matter and that sometimes it's a blessing when you don't get what you want.

Duke had his wallet lying in front of him. He unfolded it, pinched a book of stamps from one of the compartments, peeled one stamp off and stuck it on the corner of an envelope. There was something effeminate about the whole action. Very 'Dolly', as he would say. He took a pen and wrote, his wrist dotting its way across the page, fingers cramped around a black biro. The envelope was a fifty-for-a-quid transparent jobby from the pound shop. He set it on the counter with my reinforced envelopes. Seeing that they were already stamped, he offered to post them for me as he flicked through the addresses. Most were destined for across the water.

'Ask no questions, eh?' Duke said, setting them back down.

What's there to tell? Just a bit of bread and butter. An autograph business I used to run, if you want to know, inspired by the Billy Corgan picture. I just thought that if I didn't mind being ripped off, who would?

People love to pay for the illusion of things. They know fine rightly that if something seems too good to be true then it probably is. It wasn't a big operation, twenty autographs a week at the most. A hundred squid in my PayPal account.

Duke gave me a bloodsucking smile. He sat at his bureau again. I wasn't in a hurry to tell him any of this autograph malarkey. Not when everything about him I only found out through other people.

'That Callum and his missus don't know how to raise their kids,' he said. *Rich!* 'What are you doing today, anyway?' he asked me, as I got the squeezy honey down from the sticky cupboard, which last saw an antibacterial spray and a cloth when Granny was still well.

'Umm, Clint's coming for me soon,' I said.

'Dr Tree been called into surgery?'

'Aye, that's right.'

I could see what he was doing a million miles away. After all, it was my room that was beside Callum's house. He was trying to butter me up in case there was a confrontation, and I'm not saying that Callum's eldest two boys weren't cheeky little shits – they most definitely were – but Granny had always managed to live beside them in close to harmony. Then again, she was too much of a pushover.

Still, there had to be a happy medium. There had to be open lines of communication and accountability.

'Clint has a job on Low Road for me.'

'That's not far, why don't you walk it?' asked him who's never walked the length of himself.

Shut your mouth, I felt like saying, just shut up. What is it to you if Clint wants to collect me? It didn't matter. Duke never really wants an answer, he just likes asking the questions.

I squirted the honey onto the toast in a viscous spiral, spread it out with a knife to the edges, made myself a cup of green tea and went to sit in the living room with it. I looked at the curtains, still half shut, the way they'd been left when I'd distracted Da by shouting at him the night before.

There were swags and tails at each side. I wondered why he

never bothered to make the house into a bachelor's pad like I'd first expected he would. The room was still floriated and out-dated, is what I mean, even with the odd piece of new furniture. Everything in the house shouted 'Granny' at me. I thought about her, surrounded by her little red napkins of chewed-up food. My bowels dropped.

Clint pulled the van up outside the house, his horn releasing a soft bleat into the street.

'See you later,' I said, putting my cup in the sink. 'I'll scrub that when I get back.'

Duke was looking at the photo of me on my third birthday, or maybe he was looking at Mum, or even Mrs Wright's arse – God knows – either way he tried to make it look like he wasn't. My so-called da: the biggest cover-up operation to walk the streets of County Down.

'That you off?' he said.

'That's me,' I said.

'See you later.'

He turned around and gave me a thin smile.

I lifted a bottle of water out of the fridge and my letters from the counter. I didn't get a chance to glimpse who he'd addressed his letter to, didn't want to be too obvious about it. And why the heck not after the scanning-over he'd given my parcels? And then I headed out.

Callum was straight out behind me.

'Scott, can I have a word?' he asked, tucking his fingers into the arse pockets of his jeans to give him the look of being relaxed, but his tense face and his shoulders, which were practi-cally up in line with his chin, gave me the opposite impression.

'Yes, Cal?' I asked him. My eyes cast over him then over Clint.

Clint looked at his phone and slumped down in the driver's seat, giving us a minute. He could read Callum's face. Knew he was serious, for once.

'What's up?' I said.

'Where to start, Scott?' I hated the way he was using my name, the same way the dean had. How certain people try to assert their age, their authority, over you. You know, the way you do? Well, *that* way.

I just stood staring at him. I was waiting for Callum to tell me that I'd woken up the baby. Of course I'd apologise. I wouldn't get into detail, the details of my arse-about-face relationship with Duke needn't have been public knowledge at that stage. People weren't interested that he'd been looking at his mother as if she was something that repulsed him. People didn't care about personal, internal stuff. The only stuff I've ever actually cared about.

I wasn't at uni anymore. I had to live beside these people. I'd say I was sorry, that it was a stupid argument and I'd accept his crossness and we'd shake hands, because Callum always seemed all right. It wasn't his fault his sons were little shits, I thought.

'It's my garden,' he said and I looked over.

It looked the same as ever, a concrete block, a big monolithic tree in the middle that would cast leaves all over the place come October, and he'd always rake them up, not wanting Granny to slip – as I said, Callum was a decent spud. *Was* a decent spud.

'What is it?' I asked.

'Now, Scott, don't act daft,' he said.

'I don't know what you're on about.'

'The *back* garden.'

Garden again. It was a bit up-yourself to make out we had

gardens. I looked at him. Callum was looking back like he was having none of it, like I was messing him about on purpose.

'That was a right racket last night,' he said.

'Oh I know. About that . . .'

'It's none of my business.'

'It was Granny's anniversary and . . .'

He put his hand up.

'Don't want to hear it. It's none of my business what it was about.'

'Of course not,' I said.

He knew who Duke was all right, that's why it was me who was getting the earache. That's why he was stammering as he spoke.

'It-it's just revolting what you did, and I-I know you have your issues.'

'What like? What issues do I have?' I asked him.

Did he mean because Granny had been sick?

'But you don't go and fill a bag full of dog shit and throw it into a garden where children are playing. Who does that kind of thing?'

'What?' I started to laugh.

'It's not funny, if one of the kids touched that they could be blinded.'

'Really? Does dog shit do that?'

Callum was turning his nose up, his lip curling at one side.

'Yes, really. What's wrong with you, Scott?'

'This is just so . . . cray,' I said.

Clint beeped his horn, harder. He nodded at me. I was on his time now.

'Cal, look, I've to go to work,' I said, slipping past. 'We don't have a dog, I'm allergic to them . . . and to cats.'

I don't know why I felt it was important to add that bit. It could've been cat shit. Maybe.

Maybe Callum was an expert in all things shit, like Da was in all things politics. Everything is shit, Callum. Maybe that's what I should've told him. He was shaking his head, releasing short huffs of breath, looking at me like I was something he'd trodden in. *See? All shit!*

'Aoife put it in the bin. I told her she shouldn't have. Should've flung it back over to yours.'

'It wasn't me.'

I got into the van. Something told me he wouldn't be going to the door to ask Duke if he knew anything about Shitgate. It could've come from the other side. I was angry how glaringly obvious to everyone it was, how little my own father thought of me, that they all used me as a scapegoat for their own childish antics.

Clint asked nothing about it. He drove up the road past the filling station towards Low Road, he stopped at the post box on the corner so I could drop off my letters, then we pulled over outside a big fuck-off house. It was the old manse. Clint had a look at the trees he'd promised to cut down. Some were tangled, had grown their roots and branches around each other, and he'd decided it was a two-man job when he'd been out to price it up days before.

I could see nothing wrong with the garden. 'You're lucky to have the playground, and the sea is as good as a garden,' the people in our street would say to us kids – when we were kids. Those parents and guardians with their children climbing the walls out of boredom, and the roads busy enough to make the dander to anywhere exciting a deterrent.

The sea could be dangerous when unsupervised. The playground was always filled with broken bottles, and once a used needle appeared in the hand of a young girl rummaging under the rickety old roundabout for a doll she'd dropped. And besides, it was really a carcass of a playground, so to use that as a thing to tell a child they were lucky to have was just cruel.

The owner of the house, a man with broken veins mapped over his cheeks that stopped me noticing much else about him, wanted any tangled trees tore out. He thought the place should be stripped back until it resembled somewhere else, somewhere else he coveted, like how in summer people coveted Christmas.

Not me. I'm always ready for the change when it comes, but not a moment before.

The air was warm but not too warm. The last couple of days had been the strangest, but at least the rain held off while we worked. I held a branch apart from its tree while he performed his incision. Clint asked me if I'd heard about the man in the village.

'I have,' I said.

I thought about Larry and decided I'd call in on Granny later that day. Generally, I didn't see her every day, there were lots of events and outings planned through the fold. She had a better social life than ever in the summer. I wanted to see if she was okay with her son's behaviour at the meal. But was it really so different to any other time in his company? Maybe she never even registered it. Maybe she just did as she pleased and stopped caring about what he thought.

'The man in the village, he was called Bertie Beattie,' I told Clint, not that he was too interested.

I got the feeling that Bertie was no more a real person to Clint than he was to me, he'd been trying to make conversation although he was even more submissive than me, but much less of a saint. I had Callum on the top of my mind, on top of everything else. *Callum-bag-o'-shit.*

'D'ya hear what happened to him?' I tried to lure Clint into a chat. God, I missed Klaudia for that!

'Oh, killed in his garage. They haven't got anyone for it.'

'Yep,' I said. 'It's mustard,'

He looked at me from behind the branch he'd been sawing at the join.

'Mustard indeed,' Clint stated.

I had no idea if he was being sarcastic, like when he'd asked me last April if I'd done anything while he'd no work for me.

'A few shifts in the Nurseries and a wee funeral,' I'd said.

'A wee funeral,' he'd repeated.

His tone never changed, not like when Duke would repeat my words, throwing them back at me to try to embarrass or shame me. Duke always added his own shade to the words and made them ugly, but when Clint did it you knew he was really thinking about the words, spreading them over his tongue. You'd said something that was making him think, making him examine you – or something like that. It made me go into myself again.

Clint never mentioned Bertie again. The rest of the shift's communications were him giving me directions like we really were in an operating theatre. Nurse Dolly Scott, I was.

We worked on into the early evening that night until it'd gone grey, though not yet twilight-grey, the night just starting to fall in. The atmosphere getting mizzly. Not enough to warrant a coat but enough to make the hairs on Clint's arms look as if they were covered in dew. The breeze that came up the road from the inky-looking sea would've made you shiver. My armpits chafed with hot-then-cold sweat.

'Look at the garden, the mixture of this month's rain and last month's brilliant sunshine must've made everything over-bloom,' I said.

'It's a mess. Believe it or not, the seasons are all messed up.'

Clint was another one with firm opinions on everything. Maybe it was best that he just shut up.

He was going to drop me home but I declined and insisted that I was 'only down the road'. Listened too much to Duke's opinions.

'All right. See you tomorrow.'

Clint pulled away from the pavement up towards the rugby club while I walked the two streets away and the sky dimmed. It lashed heavy on me in my gauzy, long-sleeved top and my shorts.

The rain caught Aoife too, who was round the corner from the filling station after doing a small shop there, pushing the pram with shopping bags over the handles making it lopsided, her two bigger boys whining incessantly beside her.

The rain had washed her mascara in black oily streaks down her face. Her arms were weather-beaten, rindy and dimpled with cellulite. The boys had their hoodies over their heads. Any other day she would've laughed embarrassedly and said, 'Typical, you forget about yourself when you have kids,' or, 'Lovely the way this Indian summer has turned out, but we can hardly complain, can we? Not after the July we've had.' But of course Aoife was in no mood to be civil. When she looked at me I felt like telling her, 'You know, whatever happened to your garden it had nothing to do with me.' But I couldn't. I wouldn't apologise for something I hadn't done. I never will again.

Aoife told the kids to run on ahead, out of my way. They were looking at me the way people do, only worse because they were so young.

It's funny what some people tell their kids. When I was a kid I was either told nothing or a pack of lies, but whatever she told them, instead of stopping me in the street and shouting, 'Hey Scott, do you still like Iron Man? What d'you think is better, *Iron Man* or *Avengers Assemble*?' there was nothing, and I realised that even getting ignored by insignificant little shits of kids could be pretty hurtful.

I went into the house and there was my sweet old pa. He'd lie on the sofa the length of *Emmerdale*, having his Larry-nap after tea. He stirred when I rattled the door chain and bristled the mud off my boots onto the mat and stepped watery brown imprints through to the kitchen.

Duke's plate was in the sink. A waxy stamp of ketchup drying in around the gristle of a chop. Hard oven chips broken when speared with a fork. Tiny leftover bits of cauliflower, bouffant broccoli cooked to be left – I've never understood that logic. 'Eyes bigger than his belly,' Granny would say. Pure wasteful, I'd say.

My cup was still there too. I gave it a wash and set it in the drainer, pillaged through the cupboards for a Pot Noodle. Something easy. Something filling.

My arms ached when I held them above my head, but nothing like at the start. When I started working with Clint I had absolutely no muscle definition. It wasn't something I'd ever wanted to try to achieve but I can't deny that it felt good to be a bit toned, a bit stronger. I felt stronger within myself. I could back anything up now. I was looking stockier too. It was all that skin of mine thickening around me. Toughening me up.

I was stirring the powder into the plastic pot and covering it over with the lid when Duke appeared in the kitchen all bleary-eyed.

'What was going on with that left-footer earlier?' he asked.

I played daft. 'Who?'

'Yer man. Callum,' he said, although he called him Colin in person.

'Said I threw dog shit over their fence . . .'

'What'd you tell him?'

'What do you think I said?' I asked. 'I said of course *I* didn't.'

He started to laugh but I could tell he wasn't quite *getting* me.

'What'd he say to that?'

'Oh, I don't know.' I was too tired to try to think about it.

'Did he not ask you to clean it up?' He started his mental probing.

'*You* did it?' I asked.

Duke ignored me, kicked grass over.

'Eejit, banging away all night on that wall.'

'You heard him?' I asked again.

'What? You didn't?'

'Well, no.'

I didn't tell him that since Kyle's parties in the student house I'd learnt to block out sound. Those parties that really were parties, with all the ones I had no interest in: the girls from class who'd never look you in the eye but would happily drink your drink, with all their talk about blow jobs, going on about the offside rule like it was a euphemism for taking it up the arse. These girls had this internal competition, I noticed that. They were always going, 'I haven't eaten a thing all day,' or else they were saying, 'I've drank *so* much tonight.'

They got on with pretending they were really 'just lads', but the best of both worlds, boys with tits. Big deal! They would've lined up in the kitchen, the girls, taking selfies as they shouted 'Prune!' so they'd be pouting in the photos. I was sick of pouts. Sick of listening to loud, vulgar conversation and the look-at-me, *look-at-me*, over-the-topness that every party would dissolve into when alcohol melted that aloofness away to reveal the needy wrecks they all were, the girls and the guys.

Actually Kyle and Farris were worse than the girls. I was just numbed to the stupid things guys do for attention. They would play their mind games all night and then, out of their little incestuous group, someone would get off with the wrong person and there would be tears and arguing. Smashing things up.

After a week or two of that I left them to it. I'd be in my room instead, perfectly drowning them all out with just two fingers plugged in my ears. And you know what? It worked bloody wonders.

'You should've told Callum his kids are shits,' Duke said.

'Oh, I don't know . . . there are no scripts for these things, you just say what's in your head.'

'He's an ignorant so-and-so. Left-fuckin-footer.'

'What did you just say?'

I peeled back the lid again, laughing. I knew Duke could never laugh at himself. It's like seeing a car crash in slo-mo but you can't put the brakes on, you don't want to put the brakes on for once. You want to see what will happen if you don't, or if you just let things take the course they were already on. Natural, like.

'What's that?'

His expression was provocative. How quick that switch can flick.

'Thought you were impartial?' How quick mine can too.

He craned his neck forward. 'Impartial to what?'

'Politics . . . religion. Live and let live?'

I looked him in the eye and raised a smirk at one corner of my mouth. He slapped it off me. After all, aggression is his language. The big guy didn't punch me – maybe my glasses saved me – but he did hit me. And it smarted.

I can be calm in situations like that and just think. I don't get particularly hotly bothered. If I see that my opponent is, I mean. And to be fair it *was* only a slap. I'd missed a lifetime of them compared to most kids. I'm not so soft as to think I was mistreated or assaulted, I've had a life of little physical contact, good or bad. That's why I think I confused it.

I'd see Aoife slapping the backs of her kids' legs at times, but I've also seen the kisses and the boys on her hips when they were far too big for it. It's natural to have the both, I think. Good and bad. Just contact. The footprints in the sand. The dragging your heels. The crawling through the desert. The missing prints. Being carried through.

My Pot Noodle slopped three quarters of its contents all over the tiles with the force of the slap, but I just nodded, just kept that smirk steady.

'Over a barrel they have us, wee bastards. You want to take their side? Be my guest,' Duke said.

'Strictly speaking you're my guest,' I said.

Who were the 'they' he spoke of? I wore an earring: it was 'right ear, right queer'. Callum was a 'left-footer' and, when he didn't like something, Da directed your words to his left bollock. Da identifies his hatred like a road map he's holding the wrong way up. It is a deep-set prejudice that sometimes comes across as a whim no one can possibly take seriously.

And all this from the man who paused to regroup his memory of which side was left and which was right when I'd first directed him into his parking lane on the Stena Line to head over the water. He is literally clueless.

That's why it was so easy for him to pretend to be relocated: he didn't know where he stood himself. He just stopped, because all around him was quicksand and he was sinking anyhow. The only way for him was down, when he wasn't using his uppers or raising his hands.

'You still hate taigs,' I said, using his own language kept for home.

'I don't hate taigs. I just hate *that* fucking taig.' He nodded at the wall that joined Callum's house to ours.

I wound some noodles around my fork, took a mouthful from the remains at the bottom of the pot. Sucked them through my teeth.

'You don't hate *fucking* taigs that much. I thought you liked fucking taigs,' I said, mouth full. 'Conor's ma told me.'

Da slammed me against the door. Put his forearm sideways against my neck to push my head up, forced me to look into his eyes, my glasses up on one side, making him blurred in part.

'I will bust your face for you, you hear me, fella,' he said.

I had the fork in my hand. Pressed it against his ribs, pierced blubber. Took him a while to feel it and when he did he looked scorched. The double murderer. He was shocked, if you can believe that. I thought, for the first time, I had a taste of what he was feeling when he killed those boys. And maybe I wanted more than just a taste.

'Now you listen to *me*,' I told him. 'I'm done auditioning to be your son.'

I turned my back on him. Duke stood there for a while. Froze. I found a can of baked beans in the larder and, in the freezer, more bread. The drawer whistled as I opened it. I gave it a good shake, took the can opener out, rattled it like mad, walloped the drawer shut. I could see him out of the corner of my eye, could hear the depth of his breathing. Then Duke took off and tramped upstairs.

I took the top off the beans. Plopped them into a bowl to let simmer in the microwave. Sauce spat. I buttered barely toasted bread, stepping over the noodle splatter to fetch a plate, one that was decent and not just half-washed.

There was a smell, you know, it followed me from room to room, it came from inside my head. Rotted banana skins. Stale blood. In the living room the sofa was still warm from where he'd been sleeping. I burrowed myself into the space. Propped myself up on a load of cushions and got tucked into my tea.

There was a documentary on about crash-test dummies, as if I'd summoned it. I watched those figures fly at the glass, wondered about whether, when it's real people, if our hands come up to protect us, or if things happen too soon for reactions. It was amazing. I was able to concentrate. My mind had an amazing clearness it hadn't had in a long, long time. It was better than meditation. Better than the medication they had me on when I was at school.

Bang, bang, bang. Back down the stairs. Duke stopped at the door with that suitcase from under his bed filled. *Ay, caramba!* He made sure he got his Salou fortnight every year while I've never left the UK. I raised myself up on one elbow to see him fumble with the door chain that was put on for Granny when she was sick and felt defenceless.

'No wonder Mandy topped herself – to get away from you,' he said.

He got into the car, the suspension taking a knock, and he drove off.

He's one lying fuck.

6 September

Maybe the dean was right all along, you *are* starting to help. You're not a namby-pamby two-bit counsellor like Da. You're a proper psychiatrist.

Yesterday I finally opened up and told you what I wrote about Mum. About her death. The questions it's raised for me. How Granny won't reply, won't say if it was an aneurysm that took her from me (like they all said it was) or if Mum took herself from me.

You seemed genuinely pleased I was writing. Two steps forward, you said.

Then today I got a letter, this one is from Deena. It's left me with a lot to talk to you about next time. You asked me once what I'd do if Deena declined to visit. If how she saw me as a person had changed. The memories Deena has of me as a three-year-old, when she was in my life. What if I am too different now?

You said this was likely, that I needed to prepare myself for it. Surely we're all different from our three-year-old selves. But maybe I'm utterly unrecognisable. A different person in a different place.

But sometimes you say confusing things that I think I understand, and then, when I get back to my cell, it changes meaning. I wonder if you said those things to me with a tilt of your head, accentuated a particular word, if I've gotten too stupid to pick up on these things.

But Deena isn't coming to visit me, not now and not ever. I shouldn't be annoyed, it's just that I had the notion that if I understood Mum better I wouldn't be able to blame her. Because I sometimes do. Even though I don't want to.

I was hoping Deena would say that Mum always had these suspicious headaches, that Duke trapped her or something. But I know that what really trapped Mum was me. You'd think it was my own fault that I was conceived! My existence, I think it makes no sense at times.

Anyway, despite your efforts 'prior to Deena's letter', I still didn't anticipate her response:

You are a very stupid boy, thinking that you can be on a hunger strike and it be plastered all over the news and me not hear about it.

To tell me you're in there for forging famous people's autographs – it was just plain EVIL. More fool me!

There are things I could have overlooked but I have sons, Scott. What example would it give to them if I started visiting you like you're asking me to? What you did I could never forgive!

My husband's VERY angry about all this.

Don't write to me again.

7 September

Have you ever stood in the shower so long you feel like you are starting to shrink?

I remember when I was little, I'd have stayed in the bath so long that my skin was all wrinkly, the way kids do, until my fingertips looked like sultanas. I remember looking at my hands when I was small, showing them to Granny when she came in to check on me. She'd sit on the toilet lid and say, 'Are you nearly done now, Scott?' and I'd try to send her away again. Granny would stir her hand around the water and say: 'Ach, for dear sake, you'll catch your death sitting in that, let's get you out.'

When she'd dry me I'd watch myself in the mirror, being shaken and buffed and she'd say, 'There now, get into your PJs,' even though it was always 'pyjamas' until I came to live with her, and eventually she started to talk like the American TV shows, like *Barney*. Pyjamas became PJs, icing became frosting, trousers became pants and nappies became diapers, when I had to go back into them.

Now I can see why I'd pissed my bed, why I surrounded my bedspread with soft toys all around the edge, so nothing could reach out and pull at my toes. Pull me down.

Da's coming-to-get-me date kept changing. I worried that he'd been in hospital so long there must've been something really wrong, because my school friends' parents never went to hospital – only their mums, and they always came back in one piece, and always with a new addition.

When they took my mum away from the stairs they took her to the hospital. She came back with her cheeks pink again, not in powder apple-circles. More subtle. Sweeps along her cheekbones. Mrs Wright read that it was good for kids to 'see the body' and she lifted me up to kiss Mum goodbye. Mum even looked better than before, still sleeping, though her cheek against my lips felt like the sausages I'd tried to eat straight from the freezer the day she fell. I never ate meat again after.

Hospitals didn't cure people. I started to think that my dad must be dead too. That they just weren't showing me the body.

Sometimes I used to stand in the shower, the dirt of the soil and the sweat stuck to my skin. Just stand there, not budging for a good half hour.

★

Da hadn't returned after our argument. It was September. He was probably back in Belfast. I pictured him calling in a favour. Sofa-surfing rather than staying with me.

I started to do things the way I wanted, not bothering to keep things clean on the surface, where people would see. I filthied the place. Left dishes everywhere. Let them grow fur all over them. I didn't clean a thing, except myself. I couldn't stop cleaning myself, as if it would do any good.

In the student house, if I was in the shower, Farris would turn on the water downstairs, usually to have a laugh, to see me traipse down to the bottom floor sopping wet. He'd be killing himself laughing – until the day I went daft. Then he never did it again.

In that house the water went from warm to freezing like a click of your fingers, but standing in Granny's shower was different: it was so steady, like the change in the bath water I barely noticed. It was fine because it was gradual. Never broke me from my daze. If someone had put their hand in under the flow they would've said, 'You'll get pneumonia, Scott,' but I was numbed to it all.

I soaped my hands. When I looked at them they seemed to be getting smaller and smaller. I stood for ages trying to summon up the energy to get myself sorted. Water was starting to lie in the bottom of the shower, it was playing up again. There were a few times I'd seen Duke with his sleeves rolled up and a plunger over the mouth of the drain, cursing that he'd have to pay a plumber. He hated to pay anything for something he could do, even if it was a shoddy job at his own hands.

I ran my foot over the drain. There was nothing obvious clogging it. I got out. Dried off. An hour or so after, I paused a game of *Grand Theft Auto IV* and I went in to take a look. The excess water had drained. A bottle of shower gel was lying there. I picked it up, greasy in my fingers, and under it was a long hair, swirling towards the plughole, stopping just short. I pinched it. It was mousey. Long. It wasn't mine. It certainly wasn't Duke's.

I took the hair into my room and set it in front of the PC

monitor. Conor's mum, I thought. What was her hair like again? Longish, I supposed. I took my notepad and I wrote a short piece of fiction: Conor's mum was in our house, she was a hooker, and a man – my da, loosely veiled – was a john. He shagged her, then killed her to get his money back. Then I closed my book and went onto Facebook.

I looked up Jasmine. I went in under a different name since she'd blocked me. All of her settings were changed, I knew that, but still I kept trying.

You say that doing something over and over and expecting a different result can be an issue. I called it having faith.

I couldn't see who Jas was friends with, if she was in a relationship, or what she was doing with her days. I knew her da had probably been advising her. I could picture him stopping her uploading any photos of the baby.

Then I read Kyle's page, which was never private. He was too stupid to think about that. Even stupider than me. He was starting a good job and yet there were pictures of him completely poleaxed, and all the pages he liked were public knowledge – slut-shaming sites, wankers in footie kits, etc. – and yet he got away with it. If I worked in HR at his firm I'd have googled him first. Sure, no one gives a shit what I think.

I started to wonder if I wished I'd finished my degree, if I should bother trying to finish the lost modules one way or another. I was sick of being outside. The last blazes of summer it was then, but I knew the cold was coming soon enough. Wouldn't I have preferred to be inside? Away from people? On a computer? Though not filling my free time with games and movies. Maybe I needed to put my feet on the ground and start walking again. Fill my stomach with fresh air. I'd got out of the way of it.

I decided I'd go to the lighthouse. The Perry's polo shirt and shorts weren't me. I liked my arms and legs covered. That day I put on a poet shirt with a waistcoat over the top. I slipped on my sandals and headed off, carrying a light jacket so as not to be caught out by the weather again.

I walked the long way round, avoiding Callum's. He was out trimming back his hedge between his house and the one on the other side of him. I notice he didn't ask me if I had any tips. He worked in customer service, I think. Callum sometimes wore a lanyard around his neck. I think it said something about customer service, or customers, or some sort of service. I can't recall.

I thought about careers, or 'jobs', as people like Callum call them. Maybe I could see what 'jobs' there were going in the civil service. Maybe he was a civil servant, our Callum. Maybe I needn't mention university in my application. I could say I'd been away travelling – around China – that there was a gap in my CV but I'd get round to building up a career. Maybe Clint would write me a reference and I could doctor the dates. I'd get into politics, just what exactly I didn't know. Da wouldn't be there putting his two-pence worth in.

I was by myself for the first time. I was me for the first time. It only took twenty-one years.

At the lighthouse I sat down. There was this base layer of clouds levitating on the horizon, the water was heading away, toward the island. The smell of salt rising from the water was intensified by the sun. In the distance, the edges of water glinted white, raising and dipping.

I watched the mums and little kids out making the most of the nice weather, the little ones out of school early for the first month of the year. On the pillars of the wall were three little girls. The wall was four-foot-high at least. They were treading it, balancing, then freezing, shouting, 'Gargoyle!' and pulling faces. Their mums were chinwagging, eyes rarely scanning their girls, like they couldn't care less. I felt like picking one of the kids off the wall, putting her into her mum's arms and saying: 'What kind of a person are you? Did you picture you could ever care so little if your child cracked her head open like an egg, or drowned in the sea?'

I didn't do it though. And I never would've done that climbing either. Too careful. I can remember when that was me. I'm still young enough to. Memories that were strong when I was eighteen are slipping. In a few years I'll probably forget going to the park with Mum altogether. This is the kind of thing I *should* be writing down, I think: memories, before they're gone for good.

I took my phone out of my pocket as if I was waiting on a call, but really, who was there to call me? I didn't feel like seeing Granny. I wanted to forget about *that* Scott, the one she expected good things from. I'd give Granny and Good Scott some space.

My finger looked like it was going to explode. I'd wrapped the hair from the shower around it and it was throbbing. Skin all red and bulging out in parts. I unwound the hair. All dried out now I held it up, squinted to examine it. Blonder than I'd thought. The hair curled around in a ringlet between my fingers.

I wrapped my finger up again and stood, got a portion of chips and went back home ignited by the heat of the day.

8 September

I thought about how Duke hated me.

I pictured someone saying to me, 'Here, Scott, you know your Da hates you?' and I pictured me saying, 'Yeah, I know. It's fine.'

I thought that I didn't care if he, or anyone else for that matter, hated me. And once you know something like that it's somehow very liberating. It falls into place – or out of place.

When I got home I went into the kitchen. Aoife's hands were two white clots pegging clothes to the line outside: white bedding billowed like a mast, tracksuit bottoms kicked away and then her knickers, three pairs of them, fluttered in the breeze. They were nothing sexy. She probably knew I was watching her, there were gaps in the fence. When looked at from a certain angle, the fence disappeared altogether.

I opened my trousers and wanked furiously into the sink. When I reopened my eyes, after, it looked like explosives had just gone off. Aoife's hands and the blue sky all overlapped with purple smudges and bright white filaments.

Is this the kind of thing you want to know? I think it is.

Anyway, after that I texted Klaudia. (Or is this it? Getting back to her?) There had been enough space between Klaudia and I, I thought. And I was right. She replied pretty much straight away after I asked her to meet up.

'This once,' she texted, putting me back in my box.

The plates beneath us had changed. I was a bit over it, but a bit stung too at any implication.

We arranged that she would come round and I arranged to have some Polish delicacies in for her. I went across to the Co-op, to its aisle that had begun to sell Eastern European food. (I'd recently noticed that the posts into town, coming in from the back roads, had the Union Jack on one side, and the Polish flag facing.)

When Klaudia got to the house she just sat in the car and I stood over the passenger door, and she said, 'I am not staying, just get in for a chat.'

So I slipped in, pissed off that I'd spent all that money on her. On meat.

'Scott,' she delayed, then she looked at me. She had her car radio on, my mum's song was playing, I couldn't concentrate on whatever it was she was saying and I couldn't reach over and turn it off either. That would've been rude. I was trying to make a good second-chance impression but my head was compressing. Someone tightening a screw. 'I find it hard to be cross with you, when I see you,' she was saying. She was sparkling.

'Then don't be cross with me at all.'

I picked my nails, averted my eyes from the radio. I couldn't look into hers, even though she was side on and I could *feel* rather than *see* her eyes on me, like heat.

'I asked you to stop texting me so much.'

'I did stop,' I told her.

Bastarding song!

'It is not just the texts. It is Facebook, twitter, the emails . . .'

'I've *stopped*.'

'I know you did stop . . . a bit,' she said. 'But now you are starting again, I just want to nip this in the butt.'

I smiled at that.

'What is so funny?' Klaudia asked. She couldn't help but smile too.

'Nothing,' I said.

Klaudia touched my sleeve, twisted my wrist to look at my hand. 'What have you done to your finger? It is all red.'

'Nothing.' I cupped my left hand over it.

'Scott?'

'Yes?'

I couldn't avoid looking at her any longer. Klaudia sucked her lips inside her mouth.

'I told you I was getting out of a long-term relationship. I am just working hard. He left me with this mortgage, you see?'

'I know, he treated you badly, your ex,' I said.

'You are treating me no better, Scott,' Klaudia said.

'But what have I really done? Why are you so distant with me?'

Klaudia never appreciated all the things I *never* did, just focused on what I *did* do. What about how I never corrected her slip-ups? As good as she was at English, she fluffed her lines from time to time. Also, I never took his side, this ex, and never told her to shut up when she was bending my ear back at Perry's with her stupid questions, when I'd specifically gone there for peace and quiet. If I wanted to listen to shit-talk I could've got a job in a bar. There were always plenty of those kinds of jobs going.

I glanced back at the house, Aoife peeking through her blinds, rocking the baby in her arms although he was getting massive and it looked more like a wrestle. I wondered what size Mya would be now. I watched Aoife until she pulled the blind-string to block me out.

'I am too old for you, Scott, and women, girls . . . they mature faster.'

I agreed with what Klaudia was saying. I just wanted a friend.

'I'm not interested in a physical relationship,' I said.

But Klaudia obviously thought a guy and a girl couldn't have a relationship without sex. Maybe *she* couldn't, maybe my da couldn't, but not me. I just wanted someone to listen to my story, to confide theirs in me. I was well-glued into the friend zone and happy to be there.

'You've got the wrong idea of me, Klaudia.'

'Do I? I don't think so,' she said, her eyes glittering without her even trying.

'Where are you getting your ideas from?' I asked.

She went quiet.

I put my hand on her headrest, let the hair unravel, darker at the roots, beside her head. The exact same length.

'Klaudia?'

'Yes?' She looked at me. Blushing.

'Who would you rather, father or son? And I don't mean for deep, philosophical conversation.'

I saw her eyes, the birth of something new in them. I didn't wait for an answer but jumped out of the car and slammed the door. Rattled the car.

Callum had been looking out of the blinds and out he came, pretending to water the husk-dry hanging baskets at either side of his door. I stood there for a while, silently begging him to say something to me. Dared him. I was in no mood for it. He looked at me then bent his head. I went back into the house.

Klaudia is on my mind a lot lately. I think she had a full life. Thirty-one is better than twenty-one. I'm sure she didn't like everyone she met in her life. I'm sure her ex-boyfriend had his version of events. For all I knew Klaudia was at fault for their relationship ending. She was sneakier than I'd thought. Maybe she deserved to be left with all the baggage.

If she'd have told me what had happened with them I'd have been loyal to her, but then I'd have wanted to hear his side too. If I'd met him and he'd said, 'Listen, Scott, she was screwing around, she was never wanting to talk about anything other than her lists of *what would you rather.*' Then, you know, I wouldn't have blamed him for doing a bunk. No, not at all. I never would've listened to a one-sided story merely salted with facts and formed a conclusion from it.

Yes, I studied politics, I know that's what people depend on, that the masses don't form an opinion, that they can be propaganda-led, that some people who are full of the gift of the gab can think through an idea and put it to everyone else, and that they'll be lazy and say, 'Sounds good to me.' People stop questioning things because they are too busy and they like having sides to take. And when they listen to both sides (the slightly smarter ones), they think, *Yes, I like that one better*, they make monsters of one side and they latch themselves to the other, although there are pitfalls with both proposals. It's human nature and I'm not going to change what it is to be human, even if it is wrong.

If people want to think that I'm a monster because of what I did, then that's fine. If they want to listen to all of my side then that's a step more towards understanding. But it's like me: let's say I hated someone, let's say that person was Duke McAuley, let's take it one step further and say that I told you all of the things I hate about him and then you said, 'He's a right royal prick.' Then I'd think you were so right, but it wouldn't make me happy, because then there would be something fundamentally wrong.

If you were saying it to show me support, I'd appreciate it. But if you can listen to a one-sided story and be happy that you're listening to gospel – not gospel maybe, whatever it is that you trust in unconditionally, and now I'm remembering how little I know about you, and how much you know about me – and then trust me completely, then you're not who I thought you were when I decided you were the right person to talk to all this about.

Because if you'd do that, then if *he* had got to you first you'd have taken his side. And if he gets to you next, you'll change teams. And once he's had his claws in, I am done with you anyway.

10 September

'Stick that up there.'

'I'm trying to.' I pressed the banner against the wall.

I got down from the chair, the foil was going slack. Blu-Tack alone wasn't strong enough to hold it up.

'I'm not putting Sellotape on the wallpaper,' Granny said.

She took the banner down and cut it into smaller strips. Then she stood on the chair again to stick each foil rectangle to the top of the door frame. There was a packet of balloons on the arm of the chair.

'I'll blow them up, Granny,' I said.

She let me. Every so often she would take one from me and pull it around her loose-knuckled fingers. Tie it in a twanging snap. The balloons sat all around the carpet and gravitated towards the edges of the room.

'Can we tie some up outside?' I asked.

Granny looked at Phyllice, her friend from next door – this was way before Phyllice died and Callum and Aoife took the house on. She was our only party guest, Phyllice. Poxy party, a *party* for Da. Phyllice paused in the middle of *her job*, which was checking that everything was straight, like she was the spir-it-level woman, thin and grey as one too, wearing a yellowy green jumper that wouldn't have been unlike the liquid inside a level.

She laughed that we should forget balloons and get a yellow ribbon for around that old oak tree out the front. There was no tree in front of our house, just a wall. The tree was on her side, sprouting out of a hole in concrete. If it could talk it'd tell some stories, that tree!

'No, Scott, son,' Granny said. 'Just keep all the balloons *inside* the house.'

Phyllice nodded in agreement. 'I'll put the kettle on and then I'll leave you to it.'

She wasn't intending to stick around once Da got to the house, she was there to give Granny a hand. Everybody used to be like that, like a chain of people all scratching each other's backs, and you didn't need to be overly enamoured with the ones further down the chain: she did for him, he did for you. No one did anything for everybody in one fell swoop and nobody seemed to ever do anything for themselves either. Except for Duke. He did just fine solo.

Granny spooned condensed mushroom soup into vol-au-vent pastries, levelled them with the edge of a butter knife and slid them into the oven. She put the flowers Phyllice had brought her into a vase in between the sarnies and French Fancies, and I got bored and went into the living room to kick the balloons about.

Phyllice popped her head around the door. 'Careful you don't knock your Granny's good Belleek over.'

'There's nothing worth anything in there,' Granny shouted. 'Nothing that can't be replaced.'

'Still, Isla,' Phyllice said.

She was absolutely ancient, probably like the ones who would've smacked Da if he was running round the neighbourhood wreaking havoc. She was a generation above Granny, covered in liver spots and didn't bother with dentures, just chewed the cud, like.

'This is not your house, young man. Your daddy's coming to take you home soon.'

Phyllice meant it as a threat, but boy was I excited. I wanted to skid along the rug and boot all the balloons in the air. I remember Phyllice getting herself in a bit of a state and Granny telling her that I was okay, maybe just 'a wee touch eager'.

'Scott doesn't know his daddy. Duke's always been *in hospital*, you see.' All exaggerated.

'Aye, hospital.' Phyllice rolled her eyes. 'Well, here-dear, I hope he's better now, Isla, for everyone's sake.'

She always said Belfast sayings that I thought were gold dust: called the hot press the 'hat press'. I'd been baffled when Granny made me help Phyllice after her fall – which, incidentally, was entirely different to Mum's kind of fall – to reach the towels down from her hat press. All three of us were small but I could climb, and so I go up there, to see folds of bed linen and numerous towels, but not one single hat. I wondered what a hat would need to be pressed for.

Here's another good one: when I made her a cup of tea, during those weeks when I was her slave – see? me helping out Phyllice to help out Granny – she dipped her finger in the tea and stirred it, like a knotty branch in a puddle of mud, and she said, 'Ach no, sure that's *cowl*! Boil the pot. Let it boil. This is only *loo-warm*.' Loo-warm. Made me think of pish-water. Took me to the fair! Still does. On good days. It's slipped into my vocab like a catchphrase from a movie only I could see.

So there was me, clambering up to her oven to boil the teapot, past her dusty 'imitation' flowers that were gathered in a vase which was made of glass, but looked distinctly milky through neglect, and had attracted algae around the unnecessary water line. Granny would've died off to see me because I was only young, and well warned away from pulling dangerous stunts like that at home. I never even climbed a tree, even the climbing frame in the park – pre-needle discovery – put me in a dizzy.

Another thing about Phyllice, while she's in my head. (It's strange – nicely strange – to have a new memory instead of the usual crap that keeps burrowing, laying and multiplying.) About a year before she left us, poor old double-edged Phyllice came into Granny's house. She was getting worse on her feet and rarely left the house, but Granny went in next door and coaxed her out. They reappeared along the wall. Granny had her, one hand under her oxter. Phyllice was wearing sensible grey-black trousers that had the shiny look of Teflon. On her feet were bright white trainers and on her back, a red coat. The hood up. She was what Little Red Riding Hood would've been like aged ninety.

Granny eased, or more like cast, off Phyllice into the space on the sofa beside me. I'd got out *My Super Ex-Girlfriend* – I'd give it a miss if you're wondering, not much cop, Sunday-after-noon filler at best.

'Oh, I know her,' Phyllice kept saying.

'Who's that?' I finally acknowledged her so she'd shut the hell up.

'That girl in that picture. She was in *The Producers* too. Remember that, Isla? Made into a video now, I saw it one day.'

I was surprised Phyllice had watched a movie at all, I just imagined her spending her days . . . no, I didn't imagine her at all.

I don't know what I imagined, but I was surprised that Phyllice knew who Uma Thurman was – even if she called her 'Urma Truman'. And she didn't just know her name (well, sort of), she knew loads about her too.

I'll not bore you with the details here. This is a diary after all, not a celeb magazine, not the like of those things that Jasmine would've had in her satchel. They always had people like Cheryl Cole on the cover, who, incidentally Jas wanted to be like so much it made me sick.

Not that Jasmine made me sick. Nor did Cheryl, although I

can't say I've put too much thought into her either. Cheryl's on the Phyllice train of people who are in the bigger picture but have not infiltrated my mind.

What pissed me off was Jasmine not being happy to be herself. Yes, that's probably it. They tried to turn girls into clones. Loads of fakery so they grew up hiding themselves. I blame those mags, in part, for why all the girls I met acted like they did.

I hated those chick mags and their articles and their airbrushed photos because they did nothing to help vulnerable girls like Jas. Because she's like me, and I know how she feels. How you can't love yourself if your parents never loved you in the first place.

'She's a big, tall girl.'

'Who is?' Granny asked, standing at the ironing board, spitting on her iron to see if it was warm yet.

'Urma Truman,' Phyllice told her, annoyed that Granny wasn't listening.

'Is she?'

'Wonder where she'd be up to, you know . . . in real life,' said Phyllice as if Uma was likely to be in the Co-op one day in town, reaching a tinned Fray Bentos pie down from the top shelf. She'd have been handy for someone like Phyllice to know. Could easily have found the hats in the 'hat press'.

So, the day of the party Phyllice kept on that I'd need to get my stuff together, as if Da was going to walk in the door and scoop me up, take me straight to Belfast. It would be my third start somewhere new, but with Duke, or 'Daddy' as he was then, it'd be more fun than old-lady talk and child slavery.

I don't know if Granny was there when Phyllice was telling me that I was going to live with Duke or not. Maybe Granny thought I was going to go, not that she seemed particularly sad when Duke didn't turn up, and eventually left me with my belly rumbling and without the knowledge then that people often let you down on purpose, not because they're sick and it isn't their fault, but because they just thought about themselves and are propping up a bar somewhere and not bothering to come to their own released-from-prison party.

I was allowed to eat the vol-au-vents then and the buns. Phyllice was like Granny is now. Couldn't get the heat into her. She always kept her coat on. Her fingers always an off-blue. Looking at Phyllice's hands made things come back to me about Mum in Mr Wright's arms, her head tucked in under his chin, but her hand swinging like a coursing wind was running through it.

Phyllice sat down at the table – the one that some ex-prisoner of Da's is probably sitting at today, getting ready to go out to a job Duke sorted for him, kissing his wife and kids goodbye, reaping the rewards of what happens when you don't run out on your family once your legs are unbound – and we all ate: Granny, Phyllice-a-glass-of-water and me. I was chirping on about Duke: 'When is Daddy coming?' And all that craic.

'He's not,' Granny said.

I saw the first of her broken looks then, my glimpse inside Conor's mum's head: the loss on top of loss, on top of loss. The giving up on rubbing the lamp because you knew wishes would never be granted again. All of that.

When I woke up the next morning every banner was gone too. I caught a glimpse of them at the bottom of the black bin outside, peeking through pastries and a splattered chocolate cake, which must've been a surprise that even I wasn't let in on. I felt like crying to see that.

Back in the living room I looked around for the balloons. She must've popped them hoping I'd forget that notion of hope myself. There were the odd dots of Blu-Tack stuck to the door like after the Christmas cards would come down. They were little reminders, stuck on the door he should've walked through, to remind me that he did exist: Daddy, this man there were no photos of anywhere.

There were family photos in Granny's albums, white hemlines down the sides from being torn in rage. My grandda had ripped Duke out of them.

I picture any photos of me gone the same way now.

And Duke started the whole thing, then Klaudia ran with it.

Their lies were a snowfall that wiped out our footprints.

12 September

Everyone's talking about Ian Paisley dying. In a funny way I think they're grieving our past.

He came around in the long run. Gave it everything and then surrendered.

I picture Duke sitting at his bureau, feg stuck to his lip.

I'd be saying to him, 'Paisley did the right thing . . . at the end of his life.'

Duke'd say, 'Aye! He did, true enough . . . he died!'

Because despite all his peace talk, you see, Duke never really wanted it. Sometimes when you're given a gift you need to force a smile and at least pretend you're happy. If he wanted peace he'd seek it with me. But he won't.

So Duke McAuley can sleep well.

The bigot.

The instigator.

Triple-turned hoor.

13 September

Klaudia never changed her email address. When I emailed her it never bounced back like it did with Jasmine, saying that there was an error.

Finding out who Klaudia was talking to was going to require her password. 'Poland' was wrong, then there was 'Maciej'. She had another brother too, but I knew that Maciej would've pipped him to the post by dying young. Put him at the top of her list.

Which would you rather, your alive brother or your dead brother?

Dead, I pictured Klaudia saying.

I imagined her looking over my shoulder while I looked at the screen.

Wrong, she laughed when I got the message saying the password was incorrect.

Think, Klaudia whispered in my ear. *Think, think.*

She made a low whistle, like she was beckoning a cat.

'Marmolada,' I said.

Hmm, you'll just have to give it a go, Klaudia said.

It worked. That dumb cat of hers.

Two new emails were still in their virtual envelopes. A promotional message from ASOS and some skincare thing. I looked through her spam: PPI reclaim, the generic bingo and Viagra nonsense. A dating website mentioned her by name: 'Renew your membership, Klaudia. One month's free trial,' it said.

I went into the site and looked around, it was asking for login details. Again she had 'Marmolada' as her password. There it was, her profile, from around the time she split from her ex. She'd signed up to find someone else, but I couldn't see any messages she'd ever sent, just ones that had been sent to her.

'You look gorgeous,' one said. They were recent but she hadn't opened them. I sent a message on her behalf, changing her email address to the fake one I used to cyber-snoop, then I felt bad and shut everything down.

I didn't feel like writing or playing a game. I looked at my photo of Corgan with his faux signature, then, bored – or fan-boying – I lost sight of myself, took the scissors I used for trimming photocopies, and cut my hair. Hacked it short enough so that I could then take a fresh blade from my bedside drawer and shave it. Didn't bother with the barber, the bathroom, gel, foam or even a mirror. I'd stopped looking at myself.

Blasted the Pumpkins at full pelt.

Fuck Aoife. Fuck Callum.

I was raging that day. You see I'd received a letter from Perry's that morning to say they were letting me go, they couldn't offer me any shifts this time of year. 'Thank you for your casual service these last few months.' It was Klaudia, of course, trying to edge me out so that there was no contact. She even got the elusive Mr Perry himself to sign it. She was good, I'll give her that.

It was the time of year to get onto a course if that was what I wanted. Clint wouldn't need me most likely, he'd said. At least he wasn't stringing me along. I wasn't wanted or needed. So I just shut down. I sat on the floor and tried to clear my mind, tried to rid it of everything – work, family, so-called friends – and I did, for the first time in ages, and when I came out of my trance I had amazing clarity. Everything was brightly coloured the way things are post war.

16 September

On my phone, before they took it from me, there were photos of Jasmine. Her lily-white skin, so pale it burnt your eyes. Nipples, tight little discs. She was curled up like a cat and stretched out, like a cat too, and she'd have been smiling. She was. I promise you.

You couldn't see her face because I cropped it out in respect for her privacy.

The day I took the pics she'd texted me to ask if Kyle was about. He wasn't. Although he knew full well what was going on with me and his cousin he turned a blind eye. Jasmine may as well have been any random girl on the street to him. She practically was a girl on the street, the way her da pushed and pulled her, taking it out on Jas that her mum had gone AWOL and come back with new train tracks on her arms. He even walloped Jas with a leather belt once because her mum got arrested.

Her parents were in and out of jail. Him for his temper and her for heroin. When things got really bad, Jasmine had foster parents who she stayed with. All that shite. Sometimes the fosterers were no better, she said. She had a ring of circular scars around her left wrist made by cigarettes being stubbed out on her skin by a woman who used to mind her. 'Those were murder,' Jasmine told me when she saw my tattoo, the yin-yang symbol on my biceps, as if it was my version, my experience of pain to be inside my own skin. My cover-up.

That day of the 'photo-shoot' I sat downstairs because, although Kyle didn't care and he had his own life, Farris sometimes had too much to say for himself about certain things. Things that concerned me. Not him.

When she showed up, Jasmine was thinner than usual. She had an openness in her eyes.

'Let's go to your room,' she said, as if we ever did anything different.

I held her hand, or more like she held my fingers, the index one and the middle finger, her hand gripping them. When we got to my room she pulled the table across the door as if someone was going to burst in. I just let her. Asked nothing.

'I found this in my mam's bag,' she said. It was the first time she'd mentioned her mum without being under the bed sheets. Jasmine pulled a little bag of powder out of her pocket.

'Speed?' I asked.

'Coke,' she said. 'A change is as good as a rest, I s'pose.'

I took the bag and examined it closer. Jasmine was biting her lip.

'You saw your mum?' I asked.

Last time her mum returned home her da hit them both. The mention of her mum staunched the flow of our conversation.

'Slag, d'ya mind not? I brought this to forget all of that,' she said.

She sat at my desk, poured a little mound, took my student card from my wallet and cut two fat lines like a pro. I'd only taken pills, only with her. Coke was a different beast.

What if I had an addictive personality like Duke, with his 'brewskis' and his 'voddy'? She covered one nostril, sniffed, rubbed her nose, her eyes watering. I lingered over my table, looked at all the tat thrown on it and the other line, so alien among it. Like me: alien among my housemates, alien among the English, alien back home.

'Okay,' I said, like I'd been asked.

I didn't need to act cool or say a thing, because she knew everything there was to know about me. Still does.

Shortly after that, Jasmine was on top of me, I was clamping my hands on her breasts. People writing in magazines would call them bee stings, the ones I looked at on my phone from time to time to remind me that there was once a time when someone wanted me around them, even wanted me to touch them. She rolled us over, I was kissing her face and neck. Jasmine didn't like it.

'I'm not made of china,' she said and pushed me off her.

Then she was on top again and the sex went on longer than ever. My cock was numbed with her. Afterwards we didn't feel like lying still or talking.

I said, foolishly, of course, 'Do you want to go out?' I felt ready anyway. I took her by the hand and tried to pull her off the bed. 'Come on, let's go.'

She curled up and that's when I lifted my phone off the table, started snapping.

'Don't do that, Slag,' she said.

'I'm not taking any photos of your face.'

I got the bed sheet and draped it over her face and she held it there. She looked doll-perfect. I pulled my trousers on and buttoned them, stuck my phone into the arse pocket.

'Jas, get dressed.'

'No,' she said.

I pulled the sheet off her.

'Jas, get fucking dressed.'

That's what I said. I'm not going to start telling you lies this far in, and I don't want you to get the wrong idea – yes, that's rich considering what I'll tell you soon – but when I talked to Jasmine that's the way we talked. She was from a bad family, I was from a bad family disguised as a good one, that's the way people like us speak to each other. We dog one another.

I knew Jasmine really wanted me to say something to degrade her, but I could never forget my granny going through me once for remarking that Phyllice was an 'old bitch'. Eminem could call women all the bitches of the day but I certainly wouldn't or Granny would be so ashamed.

In primary school when Ryley would constantly gurn in my ear in class or elbow me in the back when we were playing chasies, I told Granny on her. Granny was adamant that I would never hit a girl. No matter what.

If I was out in the street and the boys from school were fighting me, or trying to rile me, I could fight them back. I didn't need to tell her or a teacher, I had to stick up for myself – never did! – but if it was Ryley, or any other girl for that matter, then no. I was not to lift my hand or Granny would lift hers and show me how it makes girls feel when they are hit by boys. It was the only thing she was heated about, and so I respected that. Trusted my reflection in her eyes.

Jasmine wanted me to hurt her, I could tell, she had cuts on her arms. But I never did until the night she arrived with the coke. That night, when I was telling Jas to get dressed and she wasn't listening, I grabbed her by the neck. She had to step up on her tiptoes to breathe.

'Get ready now, you fucking little bitch!' I spat.

Granny wasn't present in my mind that night. She was the furthest away she'd ever been. Granny was a ghost from some previous life where things were slow and bland and everyone had colourless hair. But there I was with Jasmine, her long dark hair flailing across her face. She pulled her underwear on, her top and her turquoise harem trousers, her eyes on fire. I'd given her what she wanted but she hated it. Someone had to be co-pilot. That moment was just her turn.

She still had coke in her little bag. 'What should I do with that?'

I said, 'Top up?'

She nodded, spilled it out. Slipped her feet into her shoes.

'Where are we going?' she asked.

'You'll find out,' I said.

Jasmine watched me from the edge of my bed while I put some coke up my nose, then came over and swept the rest onto the floor with the flat of her hand.

'What'd you do that for?'

'You've never done coke before. Somebody has to be sensible.'

It felt like she was a hundred years old even though she had the look about her that babies have – fresh from the other side.

When Aoife was outside the house, before her dealings with me were restricted to those crunchy looks of hers, I'd have looked at her baby – Future Shit we'll call him. Anyway, no name looks right on a baby at first, so it doesn't matter. He was like an old man or something. He was like Larry.

'He's been here before,' Aoife said and I knew what she meant. He had all the secrets of life behind those eyes.

Well, Jasmine was like that. Like she knew everything that was going to come out of my mouth before I did.

The last time I saw Future Shit he was chubby, softened, had a cherubic innocence, all big-eyed, and Aoife was out talking to another neighbour she'd suddenly developed an interest in, only to try and show that she was friendly really, just not to *me*. She'd be yarning away, looking past me like I was the camera and she was the actress trying to appear natural. I was the fourth wall. But the baby would still smile at me, even if no one else would. Well, you see, that baby used to be Jasmine.

'Get down the stairs, bitch,' I told her.

'Going, I'm going,' she said.

There was no jovial 'slag' this time. She was irate, talking to me the way I talked to Duke, saying snidey remarks, softening her voice to lessen the impact.

It was all in the delivery. It takes a thief to know a thief.

When we got to the end of the stairs we walked through the streets. Big deal, I know you're thinking, who gives a damn? But you won't understand anything else until you understand this: I'd never been outside of the house with her. It was bizarre, she tried to hold my hand and I just snapped.

'This is what you want isn't it, to stop feeling half-diluted down?'

'So?'

'Well, so do I,' I said, but I kept looking forward, had no idea where we were going but we were going to do it, do something and anything would've dissolved fast. What was there to *really* do?

Outside the pub I saw a car, a newish Honda. I'm not a car person, I didn't care what it was but the wanky personalised reg got my goat. I stopped, thought about doing something to it. It wasn't a showy car but I wanted to shit where I ate, in a way. Wanted caught? A cry for help? Was I snow-blind from the coke? Who knows. I just had this urge that I was going to do something and it was going to be momentously out of charac- ter, like maybe I'd key the paint work or kick the wanky reg off and run.

It was the first time I'd felt that urge since Freshers' Week. That night I knew people were laughing at me in the Students' Union. It was the things Duke had said to me when we arrived: 'You can't wear those clothes, that earring, people will give you a hard time, think you're a bit . . . you know? This is your chance to be a new version of you.'

He had me paranoid.

Back when I was at the grammar school, my GP recommended meditation for when I got the dizzies. But you can't always get out your mat.

I went into the SU toilets and this guy was there. He was a student too, but looked like my da in the way he stumbled into the toilets and pissed all over the floor, leaving the door open. It was his back, his shoulders, he was soaking his shoes. I felt angry, looking at him. Then he walked over to the sinks, his dick flopped over his waistband. He was tripping over his own feet. He fell at me, hands out as though he expected me to catch him. I did.

I was saying, 'Tuck your dick back into your fucking trousers!' Just like that.

He was mumbling. It sounded like he said, 'You do it for me.'

I looked around at the mirrors, caught the both of us, me looking at myself with this big guy leaning against me, his head on my shoulder. I saw him start to retch, his cheeks filling up, and I hauled him round to do it in the sink. Then it came, watery, pint after pint, then the lumps of his dinner. He was slumping down, sliding in it. I covered my nose and mouth in case I started too.

Then he looked at me, and it was disappointment. What did he want? I wasn't going to lift him. I wasn't going to make *him* decent. I hadn't gotten myself in that state. His phone fell from his back pocket and lay on the floor. I lifted it and without thinking – or maybe with thinking too much – I threw it at the mirror. Glass splintered everywhere. Then I ran the water. It piddled out, just a trickle. So I stood up on the sink stand and I kicked the faucet. It looked flimsy. Badly put together. But let me tell you it hurt like a motherfucker. I smashed up the other mirror too.

I jumped back down, certain someone would come in any second. I screamed as I hit the tiles. Pains in my toes. They were black for weeks, bruises like black mould on white bread kept surfacing for months. But I couldn't get it checked, and crutches would've given the game away.

I hobbled out of the back door and took my puffer from my back pocket. It wasn't long before the bouncers walked past with the fella, still indecent and all the girls shrieking like they'd never seen a cock before when, believe me, they see a different one every week. They threw him into a taxi, then one of the bouncers nodded at me.

'Okay, Mucker?' he asked.

'Bloody asthma,' I said.

'My sister's got that. Don't it go in seven year cycles?'

'Myth,' I said.

Then I returned inside to look at the damage, walking on the side of my foot, breathing like a Stacey in labour.

There was a group of people all standing there looking at the glass and the jet blasting out of the hole where the faucet had been.

'How do you turn the water off?' a girl was asking, while another was giving the guy's details. 'He's first-year Politics, Zac something or other.' *Bye-bye, Zac.*

I felt sick looking at everything. The smell. The pain. I had to get out of there.

But with Jasmine I wasn't looking to slippy-tit off the scene and let someone else take the rap. (That was another Phyllice saying, 'slippy-tit'! Pure Belfast gold!) I'd man up, as they say. This woman started her ignition in the car in front of the Honda, jumped back out and ran past us, Jas and I, tutting like she had forgotten something. The car was ticking over, a crappy little Citroën not unlike Klaudia's. Though I didn't know Klaudia then to make the comparison.

'Right, bitch, you want to go for a spin?'

'You can't drive,' Jasmine whispered.

'Can't you, estate rat? Thought you could drive before you could walk.'

'I s'pose . . . a bit.'

She glanced at the woman who'd disappeared inside the house. Jasmine jumped into the driver's seat and slammed the door. Was I going to stand there and let her do it alone? It was my idea. Not that she had to do it. Nobody was pressuring Jasmine, but there is only so much time when you're grabbing an opportunity.

It wasn't planned. It wasn't malicious. If anything it was the opposite of those things.

I ran round to the passenger side and jumped in. Jasmine started kangaroo jumping us all over the road to begin. I looked over my shoulder, the woman was on her doorstep, frozen and getting smaller, holding a mat, a rolled-up one for yoga or meditation, and then we were around a corner.

And I know that we were stealing the thing, and on drugs, but that reasoning was already out of the window, like my head. Out of my head. My head out of the open window.

I shouted back in for Jasm;ine to slow down. 'You're going to topple this thing!'

So she did, she had to because we lifted off. At least that's what it felt like. We were in the centre of Newcastle.

'Should we get onto a main road?' I asked.

Jasmine laughed. I leaned out, I wanted to fall on the road, I wanted to feel the hurt, but obviously nothing was ever fast enough for Jasmine: never fast enough, never hard enough, never exciting enough. I'd never managed to lasso the moon for her.

We drove around like that, down the dual carriageway, hitting a hundred miles per hour. Then she slowed and I climbed back in the window, realised highs like that don't last. Jasmine slowed down too, when she saw the sirens in the distance, the blue lights gaining on us, whether it was us they were after or not was another matter. It felt like we were untouchable, they would see the way she'd pulled the car horizontal across both roads.

Jasmine jumped out and ran into the housing development at the side of the road. I could've tried to do the same but I just froze like the mat-woman had who'd watched us drive off in her car. The police stopped, got out of the car and I slid myself over. Sat in the driver's seat. Wrapped my fingers around the wheel. Became the pilot.

They let me off with a caution. I had to meet up with the 'victim'. They called the programme 'victim-offender mediation'. The mat-woman worked with troubled teens. A social worker. with heavy eyelids and a knowing smile. Said she knew I didn't normally do that kind of thing. Being in uni saved me. She didn't want me to have a criminal record. She even gave me a hug in the police station and I stayed rigid, stared at my laces, learnt how to fidget. It was another week before the meeting with the dean, before Da could get over to collect me. I wanted out once I knew I was going. Sugar bear was coming in the morning to take me home.

Jasmine's da walked straight into my room the night before I left. I was packing up, boxes Da would just end up looking at and laughing and saying: 'Just pick the one, there's no room in the car.'

I thought her da was somebody to do with the landlord until he pulled me off my feet. I was nine and a half stone dripping wet then. He rammed me against the door and accused me of being a sicko. Then I knew him. They had the same face shape: hearts, wider at the forehead, tapering chin.

'I'm leaving,' I told him.

'You're fucking right you are.'

He slammed that wide forehead into mine. I fell to the floor, my glasses cutting the bridge of my nose and grazing his forehead. I thought he was going to mention the car, but he didn't.

'This is where she's been coming? Here?' he shouted at me.

I watched him, he was looking around my room and all.

'If I thought this was going on before now I'da pulled the carpet from under you, boy.'

He lifted my boxes and tipped them all over my floor.

'You don't call her. You let her get on with her life.'

'Why? So you can continue to treat her like shite?' I said. 'You're a bully and her mum's a waste of skin!' I shouted.

He pulled me off the floor by the scruff of my jumper and dragged me to my feet. My hands on his. 'She's getting rid of it!'

He gave me a punch in the gut. I looked up from where I was crouched, winded, watching him linger over the bed like if he had petrol and a light he'd have set the whole thing on fire. I pictured him punching Jas in the stomach. Killing our baby.

21 September

I looked at the dating site, at the men. There was one who stood out: Todd, username HotToddy. I'd used Klaudia's free membership to find details about him. HotToddy was thirty and described himself as being a bit of a techie geek: 'small but perfectly formed'. So I sent him a message.

'Hi Todd, would you like to talk?'

That's how that part started.

25 September

In October, in the hospital, Duke stood over me like he had everything worked out. It wasn't like he thought. Wasn't black and wasn't white.

It'd been a couple of months since I'd seen Klaudia. One whole month of talking to Todd before we agreed to meet up. I'd done some research on him: Todd had a whole other life. On Facebook he was a doting family man. On email he was a slag.

Klaudia had sent me a message to say that her mother was sick and that she was going to go back home. Had no idea when she'd be back. That's why I met Todd there. At Klaudia's.

'I will call you when I return, Scott,' Klaudia said. She seemed to be softening.

The clocks had just gone back. It seemed really dark for eight o'clock. For a moment I wondered if I even had the right house. There were steps up to the door, wooden barrel planters, one at each side. Klaudia's spare key was in a plastic faux-stone in her rockery, the type that was easily purchased from the Betterware catalogue put through our doors each month. The 'stone' was obvious-looking. I was disappointed in her predictableness, not that I hadn't went prepared, just in case. But her way, the Betterware way, looked more fluid and natural to anyone, should they be watching.

I casually let myself in, even took time to kick the mat against the step, for authenticity. I could be the new beau, or a brother. I could be Maciej, back from the dead.

I was surprised that lights were on, and not on a timer – Betterware sell them too. They're foolproof! It was then it fell into place for this fool: Da had been pulling her strings, getting Klaudia – *my* so-called mate – to tell me that she'd be away. It was why she was (out of the blue) being nice to me. He knew it'd get me going, that I'd think that she was choosing our friendship over whatever nonsense she had going with him. It'd been *her* who'd texted *me* in *his* game. It was Klaudia he'd been using as the pawn.

Poor Klaudia.

Poor me.

Poor, poor wee Scott McAuley . . . whoever he ever was.

I thought that if she showed up, walked through the door, dropped a cup and smashed it at the shock of seeing me, the way women do in scary movies, that I'd have to make up a story that I only called to check on her. In the end I didn't say anything at all. Not even when she was asking me, 'Why, Scott? Why?'

But you'll want to know the details, it's all I've been asked in here by those who aren't repulsed, who think their reasons for their crimes are better than any I could ever have. Surprisingly, criminals are a judgmental lot. Surprisingly, they want to have some sort of sorting system of crime and respect. The two don't always go hand in hand, let me tell you.

Of course, I don't reply to questions about that night, it's all between me and you. When the time is right.

Klaudia's house wasn't how I'd expected it. There were a few photos but none were in black and white like I always pictured her, just your everyday average ones of people who I assumed were her mother and brothers. There were some kids, girls, maybe nieces back in Poland. There was Klaudia, arm around a little blonde girl. The house wasn't particularly stylish. Just like my house (Granny's house) the sofa was swampy with throws and cushions. She hadn't stamped anything with herself. It felt like a rental despite her mentioning the mortgage umpteen times. But then again, that could've been another lie.

Of course I'd never been to Klaudia's home, I was purely someone she met in safe places: outdoors or in her car. Nowhere I could do the steering. She was always that scared. Scared or unsure. I could see it then as I stood in her living room.

I could hear it too: walking about upstairs. Feet shuffling. *Fear*. Music murmuring. *Confusion*.

One step.

Two steps.

On the wall, on the stairs, was Klaudia's mask collection. There was the one she bought the day we met at the lighthouse. It looked at me with its empty stare.

Three steps.

I lifted it down from a nail that was hammered in, hammered bent into a hook. Held it in front of my face.

I began to feel like a collage: bits of everything making up my face.

Four steps.

My hands started to shake.

Five steps.

That's when I got the dizzies.

Terry Sawchuk was a Ukrainian-Canadian ice hockey goalie who never wore a protective mask until they were compulsory. On his face he had hundreds of stitches. The guy's face was like it had been taken apart and put back together. Full of scars, like patchwork. Imagine that . . . imagine loving something that much that you would let it destroy you.

Terry couldn't sleep at night because he'd been injured so badly over the years. He walked with a stoop from all that crouching. Thing was, there was no one to replace him with, so he just kept going.

In the end, what happened was that Terry was fighting this

guy he had always considered a pal. They had a tussle. Something and nothing. Terry fell on this guy's bent knee. Later, aged forty, he died in hospital from his internal injuries.

Sometimes I think about him. When I'm not thinking about Klaudia.

After. After all that, I left Klaudia's kitchen door ajar and went out to her back garden. Marmolada ran past me, my heart still making mad thud-thud-thuds in my chest. I wondered about my inhaler. If I should've brought it.

I entered Klaudia's garage, where her Citroën was held captive. I walked past the car, past this metal stand screwed to the wall, housing used pots of paint and boxes of books. I cracked the front garage door up, up halfway and I watched the orange glow of the street lights on the ground outside. After a while HotToddy's car pulled up, throwing its shadow forward, the purr of its engine dying. I heard his door open and shut, the bleep of the car being locked. My phone in one hand, I pushed the box on the nearest shelf onto the ground. Books clattered on concrete.

'Klaudia? You in there?' HotToddy called out. He stopped in front of the garage door.

I stood back, tucked in beside the stand, my spine tingling. I could peer down, see his bottom half, indigo jeans and shiny espresso-coloured shoes. All tarted up, aftershave potent. You could smell him before you saw him. I put my phone on speaker: Klaudia's message from that day I was late for her. 'Hi, babe I'm here waiting for you, hurry,' came her voice, so different in tone from when I last heard it. This time clear. Assured. Fearless.

'Coming now,' Todd said.

He cracked the door up rest of the way, much noisier, more reckless than I had anticipated.

Todd walked inside. He stepped over the books, head turning this way, that way. Walked straight past me. He wasn't as short as he'd let on. HotToddy was at least two inches taller than me. You don't gain good overall perspective from dick pics alone.

Then I stepped forward so that I was behind him. Todd turned around. Face to face. I pulled my knife on him, he was able to wrestle it – not away from me, because I had the grip of a madman – but against me. That's how I got cut. Warm, warm blood.

HotToddy's face changed in each millisecond of the struggle, from shock to fear to the relief that was pulsating in his pupils, but he didn't count on what came over me. I found my strength, turned the knife back into his gut. He clutched the handle, grunting like he was breathing through a gas mask.

I was able to reach for the jump leads lying limp over a box – Klaudia's car-repair kit. I was able to wrap them around his neck, around my fists: throbbing, aching, going as red as his face and seeing the veins in his neck, his temples, forehead. It felt like everything was veins, blood, pumping, pulsing, him and me both. The smells. Hot blood and steaming shit. Somewhere, rotted banana skins.

I pictured myself no longer as a grain of sand in a wall, but as a whole wall, strong in one moment then crumbling down on the ground. Spilling. I felt that same release of being built and being simultaneously broken.

There was a rag in the repair kit. I could tell Klaudia had been using it to wipe her dipstick after oil checks. I pressed it against my side, stemmed the wound as best I could. The sight of the blood made me heave my guts up on her pavement. Sour water, blanched spaghetti.

Sick dribbled off my lip, then blood, all over the pavement. I felt my way back to Klaudia's kitchen door. Could barely lift an arm to wipe my face on my sleeve. I had to crawl up the stairs.

One step.

Two steps.

And so forth.

Heave myself back to her.

In bed she held me in her arms. I whispered I was sorry for what I'd done. She was still warm. I put my head on Klaudia's chest. Her hand I placed on my head. I tried to picture her smiling, giggling, sitting on a crate seat in Perry's. That first day.

I closed my eyes. I thought we'd go together. That it was the course things should've taken. *Klaudia, why did you tell me you wouldn't be here?* I asked her, but no sound came out of me.

5 October

Last time I wrote to Jasmine I asked her if she'd forgiven me. Against your advice. She wrote back. I got the letter today. She can never forgive me for the last year, she says. I've never hurt her, as such, but I've let down the baby. Our baby. Mya. Our free-falling happy accident.

Fourteen months old now, she is. Walking. Talking. Everything.

Jasmine's getting her own place. Though it galls me to say it, she's having another baby.

'I'm with a nice boy. Jonny's eighteen and he works full-time.' That's what she wrote.

She'll be a teen mum with two kids. She won't be sending me anything again, she's been given the chance of something normal because Jonny's family are all close, so she says. They've taken to her.

I hope she's happy. I hope she's telling me the truth. Actually, would it even matter if she wasn't? Is anything real if you can't picture it, if you didn't see it? Can we pretend none of this happened? Wipe the slate, like?

Jasmine has dinner with them on Sundays. Jonny's mum is taking her shopping for a second cot and Jonny's sister is always around – she loves our daughter. Mya has an auntie who comes round to watch films. They paint each other's nails, Jasmine and Jonny's sister. That part made me cry. Chlorine tears swelling in my nostrils, falling off my face and wetting her letter. Back to gurning over nothing.

Jasmine said she was excited to have a new start, it would come for me too. But don't write because she doesn't want me to jeopardise things for her. Jonny will be dad to Mya because she doesn't want what we both had: jailbird dads.

I've read her letter twenty times at least. But now I'm going to put this page with the rest of them under my mattress, with the birthday card from Granny.

I don't blame Granny for staying away, she is reliant on Da and he likes to drive alone, as we all know. The card she sent me made me feel like I'm still a child. It said: 'Love, Gran.' She's allowing me that, the noun, not the verb. Dutiful to the end. But then, she never visited Duke either. Maybe she'll be there for me, for Mya's sake. Maybe there'll still be time. Even a little bit of it.

8 October

Probably loads of prisoners feel the way I did at first, that they should keep their heads down and get on with it, do their time as quietly, as inconspicuously as possible. I mean, that would be the norm, wouldn't it? But not me. Not anymore.

Have you noticed?

As time has gone on things have changed, like everything. It's the only constant, isn't it? That everything changes? It's evolution. It's the circle of life according to Duke's mate and cultural guide, Elton John. Him and his songs about love that Duke's never known or felt his whole life though. Lived it in four minute blasts, sung it on the road.

Elton is a homosexual married to another man, they have children together and that is acceptable to Duke because Elt's rich and famous, yet when Iris Robinson told Stormont that being gay was viler than paedophilia, Da had rhymed all through that Christmas dinner that she had a 'fair point', that 'two Beiruts' shouldn't be allowed a family.

And even Granny, who by all accounts had long slipped from the soapy hands of youth, said, 'That's a disgraceful thing to say, let alone think. They're hurting no one, Edward! A loving family is a loving family. That's like saying it is impossible to love someone you're not a biological parent to.'

I even said Elton could adopt me if he liked. What a gifted life! Much better than most. But Duke was adamant that Iris was right, about that anyway. *Here's to you, Mrs Robinson. Duke loves you more than you will know. Woh-oh-oh!*

It was greasy territory. Duke wouldn't cut his tongue loose all the way in front of Granny. But Elton? He had the choice to live his life like a human being with rights, to be loved and give love if that's what he wanted. He had the *means*. See?

Ah, circle of life. My mind's going around the same. I think it must be the hunger.

Today they sent someone in to make me eat. There's been a kick-up, as you well know. At first I saw you more because of it, and now I see you less. The human rights people have come out to say that I should have the right to strike if that's what I want. The doctors say no. The courts say no. You won't say who you're in agreement with.

Even Klaudia's dad has written to me, appealing to me to eat, that he has still to sit before me and speak about Klaudia. He wants to show me photos of his little girl when she *was* a little girl, photos of her and Oskar – oh, and Maciej too – and that I may not know this but Maciej took his own life. He was playing a game of Russian roulette with his friends. He got his hands on his dad's gun. So now I know, though now I don't care. 'Such a waste!' he wrote. What I need to do is to *not* waste my life too.

As a police officer for thirty years, Klaudia's dad sat every day facing killers in his work and he saw that they were human, 'even when they tried to be otherwise'. He saw me in the court when his 'baby girl's killer' was being tried. 'You have a good side and I want to appeal to it.' Yeah.

Mr Banasik hasn't been jaded or broken by the things in his life. (Like you, in a way, but you have the beginnings of it in your eyes, I hope you don't mind me saying.) He has faith that if we were sitting opposite I would tell him – what exactly? Well, you know it's like blood from a stone most days.

Mr Banasik isn't expecting a reason, because there *is no reason* why he and his wife had to take their daughter back to Poland in a box, at thirty-one years of age. No reason for her tarnished homecoming. There is nothing that can make him understand, nothing can bring her back.

'You look like a lost soul, Scott. And I feel sorry for your father because he has lost a child too,' he wrote.

So, apparently Duke showed up for the sentencing. He must not have ingratiated himself with Klaudia's mum the way he'd been like a limpet on Conor's, or they would've seen the full range of his hatred for me.

I still remember Duke's words to Conor's da: 'You're just right to invite family only, I would too.'

Maybe Klaudia's dad is right, maybe I am lost. But Duke, I'd argue, hasn't lost a thing. You can't lose something you've never had – people say that. By that same token, you can't lose sometime you never wanted. I don't even know why Duke bothered to show at court.

It was a surprise to hear that from Mr Banasik, especially because I still kept my head down at that stage. I didn't see any of them. Identified with my shoe laces, felt nothing, drowned the lot of them out. All of that there.

I've kept his letters though. I look at them from time to time. I don't want to commit, to tell Mr Banasik to 'pop on over from Poland' and then, when he gets here, end up bottling it, end up refusing to climb down and look him in his eyes.

He's shown me kindness and, though I was searching for it everywhere, now that someone has given it to me (the most unlikely person, I would've thought), I don't know what to do with it.

9 October

I told you I don't want to complete my degree after all.

For a while it seemed important. I was going to get out of here in fifteen years, I'd still be a relatively young man. I could get a job. I could have a family. Mya would be old enough to make up her own mind about me. She'd have more time with me than I ever had with Duke. It'd be fine.

But hope faded the way muscle matter wastes. A lack of food does funny things to a person: the body starts to eat itself, the stomach rumbles, then you don't even want food anymore.

If you ate you'd be sick.

What am I striking over? What are politics anymore? Politics are nothing. Nothing is politics.

When you get to a certain stage you can look at a certain spot on the wall, in between your blinks, until you stop seeing, feel nothing. Everyone says they want nothing to do with you, and then you stop feeling like you even exist. It doesn't matter. I don't matter. Most people out there in chat rooms would agree. They were always quick to blame.

When Klaudia's dad first wrote to me, I believed in myself, when I wasn't too weak and I was allowed to go outside an hour a day. I would look ahead, shoulders relaxed, jaw loose. I was a different person. Someone nobody could break.

If you're too broken, people stop trying to fix you.

Then yesterday Eric came over to me and spoke, instead of sneering his usual song 'cooopycaaat' as I walked past, and banging me with his shoulder, or getting the lackeys he's accumulated after years in and out of this dive to do the dirty work for him.

Eric's well taller than me, broad as he is long.

'I've been trying to talk to you, boy,' he said, popping his hairy knuckles.

'Talk,' I said. It came out more like a question.

'Yes, talk. You know . . . where words come out of your gob?'

I looked at him. 'Do it then.'

He pointed one of those hairy fingers at me. 'Don't you get snottery with me!'

He lit up. He smelt like Duke's car.

In here it's how they get in the good books. It was always the same, even on my placement year in the council offices, smokers got privileges: smoke breaks, a chance to get together, to be part of a clique. The things that killed people were always the things that made them feel most alive, most aware of breathing, of their insides, until they caused a big mass in their throats and they had to be fed up the nose by a tube. (And here am I waiting to do the same, and thinking about Granny and how I never would've chosen her life – how her life didn't seem worth living to me).

'Stop blowing your smoke in my face,' I told Eric.

'Ignorant wee fuck, aren't you?' he said.

'Do you mean ignorant, as in the dictionary definition . . . or colloquially?'

It's the best way to speak to people like him, zero-O-levels Eric.

'You're a right smartarse, aren't you? I suppose you had to be, under it all. Smart people can act bloody stupid.'

'Ah-ha,' I said. 'Put you cigarette out or I will.'

'Jesus,' he said, but he did stamp it out.

I didn't expect him to listen, but things have changed. I have.

'I don't know whether to shake you by the hand or sue you for copyright,' said Eric, then he laughed.

I put my hands on the small of my back then arched it. 'I'm bored. So bored.'

'McAuley?'

'Yep.'

'Could you not've taken the rap for Bertie Beattie? You were going down anyway.' Eric added, 'What you did . . . that lovely wee Polish girl, and that fella, served for this country, three tours of Iraq.'

Todd left that off his pulling profile. Not that it made a jot of difference. I thought girls were supposed to love soldiers. Them and firemen. He'd missed a trick. I probably wouldn't have chosen a soldier to mess with, if I'd known, in all honesty. But it's ended up working in my favour. A soldier, hard as nails. Nice one, McAuley, you little psycho.

I shrugged at Eric. 'Why'd you do it? Why'd you kill Bertie?' I asked him.

'Just a theft gone wrong. Had some good shit in his garage, like.'

'I asked you, why did you *kill* Bertie?'

'Fuck. These things happen when you do what I do. Always carried the knife on jobs, never had to use it before. Truth be told he walked out on me, scared the shite clean out. It was a reflex thing.'

'Fight or flight?'

'Aye. That thing!'

'So you didn't know him?'

'No. I did . . . used to be Beattie's window cleaner.'

Eric spat on the ground.

'Ah, nice career move for a thieving bastard.'

He laughed.

'Well, give us your excuse, McAuley.'

'Don't believe in them,' I said.

I went quiet then. Dizzy. When I woke up in the doctor's room I had to wonder if Eric had decked me, but then the doctor stepped forward, said it was decided that I couldn't go outside anymore. I'd be confined to my room unless I ate, and the tube was coming. I was going to be fed whether I liked it or not. They wouldn't have me fall down and get them get sued. 'All red tape now, all politics.'

'You have that right, doc,' I said.

The doc asked me if I'd read about Ian Brady the other month, been hunger striking for over a decade. The doc probably thinks all us killers – cause that's what I am now, I'm well reminded – get off reading about sickos like Brady. I don't. Clearly not as much as the doc does.

'No?' He was looking at a random spot on the wall as he spoke. 'Brady was being transferred within a mental hospital. He claims twelve officers pinned him down and broke his wrist. He wants out, into a prison.'

'I'd have broken the other one for him,' I said, 'and his ankles. At least. Kathy Bates in *Misery*-style.' And so forth.

That's all I'm going to say about in here, in here – in this book, I mean. Maciej came into my mind then, the photo on Klaudia's coffee table. I could see him in a circle of mates all spurring each other on, spinning the barrel. Sure, wasn't every day Russian roulette?

I decided I could never see Klaudia's dad. It would kill me even deader than I already was.

15 October

There was only one street in town that I didn't know like the fit of my bed. Before it was Klaudia's, that street was Hunter's. Hunter was in my class from year five onwards, when we were mixed up and I was taken away from my friends, put in with him, Saul and Isaac. They were already tight as cells in their gang.

Somehow, despite all that mixing, Ryley still sat beside me. Thick, dirty, annoying Ryley. The P4 teacher must've told the P5 teacher that I was the only one who didn't complain when Ryley would pick her nose, even though I've never had a strong stomach, especially not for big stringy, phlegmy snotters. Anyway, it went on like that, stuck with Ryley all seven years of primary school. My longest relationship.

As if it wasn't bad enough to have her scratching that nitty head of hers all over my school jumper sleeve, when we were in the playground Ryley would chase after me, trying to kiss me, asking me to be her boyfriend, mistaking the fact that I never hit her a thump for something like kindness. For me fancying her. Because she had a tart of a ma and a big sister, and they were all man-mad. Even when Ryley didn't know what she was on about, when we were six or seven, she'd run after me shouting, 'You're gorgeous, Scott.'

That was Snotty for you. But my proper friends, from the old class, were shuffled like cards and I got the bad hand. They got new friends, Blake and Leo. Cliqued together and never around for all the times that I wanted to join in.

When I spoke, Blake would ignore me. His new mates didn't like me. They all supported the same team. I supported none. And Leo started to look at me like a stranger. Unlike everyone else, who coped with change, I wasn't resilient to people 'going off' me because . . . well, I just wasn't. I couldn't bring myself to try with the new kids. I still tried to hang on to my old friends, desperately so, and maybe, looking back, if I could've let go it would've made a world of difference to my last three years in primary school.

When we were in P7, though, playing in the playground, I was walking along the smooth sides of the bricks that poked out of the periphery, kind of sticking close to the dinner lady. That neighbour of ours. Mrs Dudley seemed not to recognise me. Still, I felt safer near her. Mrs Dudley always had two girls hanging off her arms, ones with ribbons in their hair and computers at home. Tall, healthy children. They were always the favourites.

Ryley ran around and every time she came near Mrs Dudley she'd be told to 'run along' and, 'stop flapping your gums', or 'stop telling tales'. Ryley must've seen that when your mother was the town bike you didn't get the luxury of people having time for you. These are things I didn't know then, even though her sisters all looked as different to her as I was to my da, and Ryley's brother, Joshua, the middle child of the five of them, had a Nigerian dad, and not one of them had the same last name to boot.

Joshua would've been in P5 then. 'Steps and stairs,' my granny would've said of any other family, but it would've been a sin to say it about them. Steps and stairs to where, exactly? There were whispers about them. Not every child was equal, despite what they taught us in RE. Not every child had the right to be shown patience or kindness.

Looking back, Mrs Dudley knew me full well too. Ryley had her vocal disapproval while I was just non-existent. Children of murderers, of terrorists, aren't worth wasting your breath on, even though you see them day in day out, at the filling station, buying bread in between your big weekly shops. And when she was walking past our house to let her Labrador run loose down by the sea, Granny would say, 'Hello there,' and Mrs Dudley would be all stand-offish in return, offering, 'Oh . . . hello,' as if she hadn't seen Granny. Mrs Dudley must've had worse vision than me without my glasses, I used to think.

But one day.

Because that's when things happen, not a wee bit here and a wee bit there but in one event that propels you into some mad stratosphere where you go home, when you are finally allowed to, and you sit on your bed and think about when you woke up that morning. You never thought what had happened would have. You feel awful. What was the point of getting out of bed when there were such bad days waiting to grab you by the neck? But then the next morning Granny would open your curtains, you'd pretend you couldn't hear her calling you and then she'd come up again and say, 'Now Scott, it's getting too late for this carry on. You'll be marked absent. And you've been off sick too much. You need to get yourself together.' Well, there were days like that. Some stupid spiralling days that really weren't that bad in hindsight, but all added up.

But the particular day I'm talking about was something different altogether, and then I was allowed a few days off school, and Granny didn't try to hurry me. Because I ended up in hospital that day. There was no rush to get home because my homework could wait, I'd passed my exams and the rest of the year was filler for us and babysitting service for our teacher.

Ryley had been trying to catch me. That was the beginning of the thing.

'Mrs Dudley!' I cried.

She saw Ryley swinging me about, my collar pulled so much the button was hanging by a thread, ready to ping.

'Ryley, you're choking me!' I shouted, ducking to escape her.

Mrs Dudley glanced us over, clicked her tongue against her teeth.

'Ryley leave that wee boy alone.'

I was nameless, you see.

I saw Ryley's face coming up to me, the trails of green down her lips which were pursing for me. Her eyes half-closing, lashes flickering. I pulled away.

'Stop it.'

She fell backwards. Hit the ground with a dull whack. Ryley's face crumpled into tears, her mouth open, her face beetroot. Mrs Dudley had to peel the ribbon-girls' arms from hers to help Ryley up. But she stayed down.

'What happened to her?' one of the girls – one of Dudley's pets – was asking.

Ryley was trying to point at me, one hand at the back of her head, trying to say, 'He did it,' but it was coming out in bubbles from her nostrils, slabbers from her mouth. Ryley took her hand off her head and held it out. There was the shrieking.

'She's bleeding!' one of the pets started shouting.

The two of them squealed blue murder until Mrs Dudley had to tell them to shut up.

'Go get a teacher, you,' she told me.

When I went to the staff room I opened the door and looked around the room at the adults, all seven teachers I'd had all my life. It was like I was looking at every mother I'd ever had but yet I knew none of them would mother me, none of them cared about me, just that I was quiet and good and did my work and raised the average of the year's efforts up by a point or two. Snotty too.

'Yes, Scott?' Mrs Gillingham asked me.

Her hair was short and taily at the back and long in front of her ears like sideburns, like Deirdre Barlow from *Coronation Street*. 'What is it?'

'Ryley's head's cut,' I told her.

A wave of laughs.

'There you go now, just in case you didn't already know,' my P3 teacher Miss Ambrose said to the P4 one, Mrs Fletcher.

They'd all had their fill of Ryley through the years, had enough of Ryley not bothering to learn their names: no Miss Ambrose, Mrs Fletcher or Mrs Gillingham, just a shrill 'Teeeacheeer!' No hand raised or waiting your turn. Sometimes a whiney 'Muuummm' would slip from her mouth in bad habit. Even in P7. You could just picture the chaos of their house. The gurning they must've had to do to get noticed.

Mrs Gillingham followed me outside. Mrs Dudley was on

her hunches, Ryley with her head on Dudley's white coat, a massive stain of red eking out on the fabric. I doubt she'd have been able to get Ryley's blood out of it. Probably fit to be binned after that.

Ryley looked up at me. 'He pushed me.'

'I didn't,' I said. 'I just pulled away, she was grabbing at me.'

Mrs Gillingham was glaring like a good 'un. She crouched down too, to look at Ryley's head. Gillingham turned a shade of green.

'She's going to need stitches in that,' she told Dudley, who got up and went to call Ryley's mum while I got quizzed.

'Scott, did you push Ryley?'

'Not on purpose. She always annoys me, ask Mrs Dudley.'

'How dare you!' Mrs Gillingham shrieked. 'How dare you think that you can do this to somebody else! How dare you, *Scott McAuley*!'

Ryley was staring at me with straight, arch-less brows and a pouting mouth, she was sobbing, gasping, bottom lip quivering.

'Sorry,' I whispered, throat thickening.

'Oh, Scott, you have no idea! Sorry will not cut it. What is Mrs . . . Ryley's mother going to say about this when she has to take her to the hospital?'

'My mum can't take me,' Ryley said. 'She's got no one to mind the baby. Sasha's away on a school trip.'

Mrs Gillingham covered her eyes. 'Ryley, we'll work something out, I may need to bring you, but we'll deal with that,' she said.

Mrs Dudley came bouncing back, hand swinging, big stain on her right bap like she'd been shot or Da had got at her in an alleyway. That's all I could think when I saw her.

'Ryley's mum's coming now,' she said.

'What about the baby?' Ryley asked.

'She's bringing him. A neighbour will collect Joshua and Brooklyn if you're not back by the time school gets out.'

'I doubt you will be,' Mrs Gillingham said.

'Unless they go to the minor injuries,' went Dudley.

'I think that's an Ulster Hospital job,' went Gillingham.

These details are insignificant, I think, but it's what I remember. Funny them talking about the Ulster and stitches when Ryley took mine out in that very place. I don't know . . . it's the way times come around. It's that circle thing again.

The bell had gone ages ago before. The whole school gathered around, listening to all the details of how Ryley was going to get put back together. All the king's horses and all the king's men were standing by. It wasn't as simple as up and leaving, like when I ended up in hospital and with Granny not driving.

Everything's all easy and straightforward until it's not.

Mrs Gillingham started to march Ryley by the hand back to the school. She scowled at me.

'Scott McAuley, what do you think you are still doing standing there? Come with me this instant.'

I looked up and around. The whole schoolyard was staring, sixty or so kids, at Ryley and me. Ryley didn't mind. She wasn't crying now, and though her blond hair was already matted, it was bright red at the back now. She wouldn't have been sore anymore. I was more upset than she was. Ryley's purpose was always to be looked at, whereas I hated it. My face burned. I burst into tears. I walked behind them into the school, looking back and seeing Hunter, plotting with Isaac and Saul. His disciples.

Mrs Dudley was away home to steep her coat in Vanish, and Ryley was off to hospital in her mum's new boyfriend's car. The ranch is full of people out on the sick with fake Jeremy Kyle-loving depression and Jeremy Kyle-complicated love lives. They were always at home. It was easy to find someone who could mind Ryley's baby brother.

The rest of the day I was in the head's office doing my work. Granny had been called to tell her what had happened to Ryley – whatever version of events Mrs Gillingham had construed without an account from anybody. I hadn't been asked for my version of events, not one that would be accepted. Forget the years of torment from Ryley – they all did – I was only trying to get away. Forget all the years of model behaviour wiped out in one fell swoop.

When Mrs Gillingham calmed down, she joined me to say that I must try harder not to hit. It reminded me of Granny. 'Boys don't hit girls.' For the first time I dreaded going home. Stupid Ryley from her family she called 'blended', like they were a fruit juice or something.

'How can you have a half-brother, anyway?' I heard a girl ask her once. 'A half-sister isn't a real sister.'

Ryley had gone over to Mrs Dudley. 'Aren't Sasha, Brooklyn and Joshua my sisters and brother? Molly says they aren't.'

'As long as you know they are, that's all that matters,' old Dudley-bloody-bap had said.

Sometimes I wonder at people's logic. Clint would've examined that one. I can hear his voice, him giving it: 'Hmm, half-sisters? Well, my four daughters aren't half of anything. All by the same woman.' Then he'd have covered his face with his tree-surgeon mask and went about his business.

Ryley was lucky though. Even without a lot of toys, and the fact she wore that distinctive lime-green coat that Sasha wore for years before she moved to the high school, at least Ryley had a mum. At least she had other kids to play with, to make up games with. They could play doctors and nurses. She could practice. They could play mummies and daddies, or even foot-ball – they had a five-a-side team. The kids had a dad. And if her mum didn't like the current dad, she'd get them a new one.

Life was never serious and she had loads of people who stuck up for her. Although they were the same people who called her Snotty, some people thought they needed to stand up for her.

Hunter was one of those people. When I started to walk home he came up behind me.

'What'd ya split Ryley's head open for?' he asked, stamping on my loosened shoe lace.

'I didn't,' I said. I was a wimp back then, couldn't have said, 'And what? What's it to you, loser?'

'She's his cousin,' Saul said. Cousins, like Kyle and Jasmine. It amounted to nothing in my eyes.

'Well, you aren't real cousins. You aren't *related*,' Isaac told Hunter.

'So? We *are* cousins. My mum and Ryley's mum are best friends.'

Hunter forgot for a second that I was the one he had the gripe with. It was a soggier debate than the half-sibling one. At least I understood that one. This cousin claim was pure shite. It'd be like me calling Deena's boys my cousins. By that token I could claim a family from anywhere. No one really needed to be blood to say, 'We're family.'

So I didn't just have Granny, and more sparingly, Da. No. I could say that Phyllice was my auntie. Maybe I'd tell Mrs Dudley that she was going to be my mum from then on. She was always *Mrs* Dudley even though there was no Mr Dudley. She lived alone. Alone apart from her interchangeable Labradors. When one died she replaced it with a lookalike. Maybe I would do the same with her; she had chestnut-coloured hair like Mum. She was where the hands would've landed on the clock. Mrs Dudley was my mum, though she wasn't, like Conor's priest was a father even though he wasn't. That same idea.

Nobody spoke back to Hunter. He was allowed to make up his own rules on families. He whispered in the others boys' ears and their flinty-eyed, gapey-mouthed expressions should've told me to run in the other direction.

'Listen, Scott, let's be friends,' said Hunter putting out his hand.

I hesitated, then put my hand out to meet his.

'Okay,' I said. 'Friends.'

'Do ya wanna come to mine? That's where we're all going.'

Hunter lived on the other side of the town, past the police station. Victoria Lane, recently made famous by yours truly.

Anyway, I went. Granny had never told me not to. I hadn't been invited to anyone's house since I was old enough to walk home by myself. I told myself it would be fine, even though she'd had the call from school about the 'playground incident'. Every instinct was telling me no, but the thought of being accepted, added to my FOMS (fear of missing something) syndrome, made me go.

'Why'd ya make Ryley split her head open again, Small Meat?'

Hunter meant 'tell me again', although we both knew I never told him in the first place, and he certainly would've heard me telling Gillingham at lunchtime because you could've heard a rat fart.

'She was trying to kiss me,' I said.

'So. Are ya a fruit then?' Hunter asked.

He was a joke. He'd thumped her hundreds of times for annoying him.

'No,' I said. 'I'm not a *fruit*.'

We traipsed that direction, away from school, the boys talking about some level they were stuck at on the PlayStation. When we got to Hunter's house his mum was swanning about in her dressing gown.

'Hello boys,' she said looking happy to see us, especially me. She was delighted to see me.

'Hi, Ange,' Saul and Isaac said to her.

'Hi, Mum,' Hunter said.

'Hi, Mrs . . .' What was Hunter's surname? I drew a mental blank then and I sure as hell can't remember it now.

'Just Ange, darling,' she said, lifting a wine goblet out of the cupboard and a bottle of rosé out of an ice bucket. 'Mind you, I've been called worse things. And who are you, darling?'

She knew!

'Scott.'

'Uh-huh.'

'Yep.'

'Scott?'

I nodded again.

Hunter was getting impatient, he was tapping his foot on the lino. I remember it was lino because their washing machine must've sprung a leak and the floor was bubbled up at one corner.

'Where does your mummy work, Scott?' Ange asked me, taking a sip of wine.

'She's dead,' one of the other boys chirped in.

I barely had time to look at her again when she was on to the next question.

'Goodness! What about your daddy?'

'He's alive.'

'*I know that.* I mean, what does he do?'

'He makes sick people better.' And all that jazz. That's the kind of thing I was saying.

Ange looked suspiciously at me. 'A doctor?'

'No. I don't know . . . makes bad men good again.'

'Oh right.'

I had to look away.

'Scott lives with his granny,' Hunter said, reaching three Wagon Wheels out of the cupboard.

He'd forgotten about me. I never got offended then to be left out. I expected it.

'Of course. *Scott*,' Ange said.

As if to say 'that Scott', even though I was the only one in the school, our wee school where it was first-name terms only, except for the two Chloes and three Jacks, who had to use the first initials of their surnames. Listen, like I told you before, everybody knows everybody's business in the town. Ange worked in the Co-op. Those Co-op women knew everything going on in the town. Complete gossipmongers.

Hunter's da I knew because of his long hair and being covered in tats. Big biker fella. Face like a foot. Ange had long hair too: raven-black with bright red streaks in it.

'I bet Scott isn't going to Edinburgh with school, Hunter. You listening, Hunter? I said, I bet Scott isn't going to Edinburgh either.'

'He is actually.' Hunter threw his wrapper on the counter and stuffed the biscuit in his mouth. 'Even *he's* going.' Spitting crumbs everywhere.

'We're not made of money, Hunter,' Ange said.

'You could ask for Easter,' I said, trying to be helpful but sounding like a welt.

He laughed. 'You still believe in the Easter bunny!'

'No I don't!'

'Don't be nasty,' his mum said. 'Who's paying for you to go to Edinburgh, Scott?'

'I don't know. My Granny, I think.'

'Oh.'

'C'mon,' Hunter said, walking to his bedroom across the hall. It was all bungalows at his end of the street, compared to Klaudia's house.

Ange called me back.

'Scott, when you're going home, honey, do me a wee favour and pop those letters in the post for me. I'm getting into my pyjamas after my bath. I'll be too cosy to be bothered.'

She smiled.

I looked around. There were three envelopes on the counter.

'Yeah, okay,' I said.

'Thanks, darling. He'd do nothing for his mummy and I think Saul and Isaac are fed up doing jobs for me.'

She was quite pretty when she smiled, Ange. I could see how she'd be best friends with Ryley's mum, who was pretty too, but getting fat since the last baby and her chins were starting to dribble into each other.

'*Muuumm-meee*,' Hunter whined, just like Ryley's classroom gurn.

Maybe somewhere down their family trees they really were linked. Who's to know any different? Maybe Hunter's grotty, biker da was slipping one to Ryley's ma. Maybe Hunter was another half to add to the equation.

When we were in his room Hunter kicked the door.

'She's an embarrassment,' he said loudly enough for Ange to hear.

My shoulders sprung up to my ears. I waited for her to march in and trail him out by the hair because I knew that, if I was a parent and I bought PlayStations for kids and all the rest of the stuff he had piled thick like a boxy treasure trove and he was kicking doors like that, I'd have smacked him. I'd never had a hand raised to me at home and I still knew that he needed a hiding.

Listen, I knew he was horrible but something glued me to Hunter's bed, until he said, 'Get off my fucking bed,' and I slumped down onto his carpet.

Ange tapped her fingers on the door.

'Okay, lovelies, I'm going to get a bath now, if you need a wee go in the bucket outside, *not* on the plants, and if you need the other, go to your own houses. I don't want to be disturbed. Okay?'

Ange was the kind of woman who bought luxury hampers for herself. She was the type to light candles around the bath. Hunter raised the volume on the console to drown her out. The boys all looked ahead like they were entranced by the game. Like it was a normal day for them. I watched them finish their Wagon Wheels.

'Shake it like a Polaroid picture,' Hunter sang. 'Shake it, shake it, shake it,' Isaac sang, until they were all singing bits and pieces out of sync. I wondered if I should join in but it would've felt forced. It already felt forced.

After a while watching Hunter play and hearing the other boys complain that they weren't getting a go, Hunter told me to get milkshakes from the fridge. I got them, chocolate milkshakes, four bottles. *I* remembered me. There was no food as such: milk, butter, jam, those milkshakes and loads of paper parcels that looked, and smelt, of meat going off.

'What's that in your fridge?' I asked Hunter.

'Whatcha on about now?'

'The packages?'

'Oh, pig,' Hunter said, wincing at the screen.

'His dad does tattoos, practices on pigskin,' Isaac said, swaying side to side to check the game.

'Mum nicks the pork gone cheap in work.' You could see the cogs ticking. 'Hold on.'

Hunter paused the game, bounced off his bed like it had thrown him. He went into the hall. When he came back he had a grey bag, which he untied. It was like the bag at the butcher's in the town, which you would've seen draped over the counter, with all the knives in. Although I hated to go in, the animals cut up, hung from hooks, the sawdust floor slippy under your feet, aggravating my asthma.

The bag, Hunter spread out. Millions of little pockets of colour, a silver gun or drill, a foot pump and plug attached.

'Is that . . . ?'

'A tattoo gun,' Saul said.

Hunter had the devilment hanging out of him. You would've found it hard to like him then. I took a swig of my milkshake and saw everyone stare at me.

'What?' I laughed. 'Do I have a chocolate moustache?'

'We all have tattoos,' Hunter said. 'Don't we, guys?'

'Oh . . . yeah,' Isaac said, his eyes just a smidge too wide. I knew what Granny meant when she'd say: 'You're the worst liar out, Scott!'

'His dad did them,' said Saul, vying for top spot in the shite-actor category.

'Hmm,' I murmured.

I'm not so stupid as to have believed them. I knew what the pigs were for.

'We do,' Hunter said. 'You calling us liars?

'No.'

'We'll show ya them . . . if you don't believe us, but I thought we were mates now. Mates take your word.'

'I *do* believe you,' I said, hoping it would be enough.

'D'ya want one?' Isaac looked afraid. Obliged.

'No thanks,' I said.

I knew I was too young and that Granny hated tattoos.

'Come on. Don't be a wimp.'

Hunter straightened the leads, clicked the plug into the socket behind his pillar-box red padded headboard. Laid the pump flat on the floor.

'It's not sore,' said Saul.

'It's kind of tickly,' added Isaac.

'Nah. It's all right.'

'Get him!' Hunter shouted. They pushed me down on the bed and pulled my jumper up over my head. 'Keep him there.'

I wrestled, but they were bigger. Stronger. More of them. Hunter dipped the needle in the pot of pitch-black, the needle buzzing. He took a second to un-pause his game to cover the noise. Then he sat on my chest and the other boys held my arm still. 'G,' he wrote, all scrawly, just where my biceps curved like a half-egg. It hurt like a bastard. Then he ripped a letter 'a' into my shaking skin.

'Nearly done,' he said. 'Scott, sit a piece!'

I was crying. Sobbing. *Breaking my heart*. A mess of slabbers and tears. Everything wet, trousers included.

'Christ, look what he's done,' Saul said.

'Stop it now.' Hunter set the needle on his pillow. 'You better not've pissed on my bed.'

He pulled me off the bed to examine his sheets. I was clutching at my arm, twisting it to see.

'That's permanent, that's for life,' I was crying, or thinking, I don't know if the words were coming out or if they were just running through my mind like the feet of a headless chicken.

'Quick, put a plaster on it,' said Saul.

Hunter fetched one from the kitchen cupboard. He closed the bedroom door with his foot when he returned.

'Shut up. It was only a laugh.' He peeled the backing off the plaster, slapped it onto my arm. 'There, it's all right. Calm down now, Gurny-Bah!'

I stood up, put my jumper on. My clothes stuck to me.

'Don't tell anybody,' Hunter said, blocking the door. 'We'll say ya did it to yourself and we tried to stop ya.'

I grabbed my bag and walked out past him. I got to the back door.

'I won't say,' I said.

'The letters,' Hunter shouted. 'Scott, you've forgot the letters.'

I ran. I ran past the house where Klaudia would live ten years later, Hunter behind me, chasing. Saul and Isaac behind him, keeping themselves right, shouting, 'Stop, Scott, we're sorry. We're sorry.'

While Hunter was saying, 'If you tell I'll kill you.'

I pounded through the streets, down the hill, over the hill, toward home. I felt my chest tighten, the breath leaving me. My puffer was in my bag. I had no time to get it or he'd get me. I threw my bag on the ground. Slowing me down. Ran up the moat, cut through, a hand squeezing my chest. I was coughing, had to stop, hack my guts up on the grass: my bleeding arm, my tearstained face, my pissed-in boxers and now vomit all down my jumper. Then I keeled.

16 October

Next thing I knew I was waking. I felt my arm. The plaster was there still. I'd been changed out of my soiled clothes, into a blue gown, but the plaster hadn't been touched.

A nurse came over to check my blood pressure, she saw it.

'What's happened here? Do this when you fell?'

I clamped my hand over it. 'It's only a cut.'

'Funny place to be cut.'

She put my arm back in place and slapped the Velcro around for the fuzz to meet a million tiny hooks.

'It's a cut,' I insisted, drained of energy, feeling the tightening around my arm.

'Okay, young man,' the nurse said, watching the little needle before taking everything apart and writing on a chart at the bottom of my bed. 'You gave your granny a scare.'

'Sorry,' I said.

'It's not your fault, love.' She smiled, nodded at the bedside table. 'Smashed your little glasses, too.'

Granny looked pleased to see me awake, not that I was aware that I'd been out cold for two whole days. She took the get-well-soon card from the bedside table, which had grapes and sweets and a bottle of MiWadi. I could smell the warmth of the Murray Mint that rattled against her teeth.

Granny handed me my glasses too, but when I put them on, everything was fragmented. I only kept them on a moment to see who the card was from. It was signed by Mrs Gillingham; she must've forgiven me for Ryley's fall when I had my own. There was Ryley's signature, it looked forgiving too. Granny never mentioned that whole debacle.

'How did you get me here?' I asked, wondering about lifts to hospital. Snotty had made me think about the logistics of emergencies.

'Our neighbour was out walking her dog, that nice dinner lady with the Labrador.'

'Mrs Dudley?'

'Aye. She saw you lying up at the moat and called an ambulance for you. You've been very sick, Scott. Why didn't you have your puffer or your school bag? You need your puffer with you all the time,' she said gently.

'Is Dad coming to see me?'

'No, love.' She rooted for something to add. 'But Phyllice is making an apple tart for you, isn't that lovely?' Phyllice was making *Granny* an apple tart. It was *her* favourite, not mine. Phyllice servicing her part of the deal.

I closed the card with my finger still inside like bookmark in case I lost my place.

'Your dad said he would visit if he could. Sure, I'll go and phone him now, tell him that you're awake . . . but I don't want you getting your hopes up.'

I looked at the card again. Hunter, Saul and Isaac had all signed it, scrawly, awkward handwriting, in permanent ink.

28 October

Duke thought that I *was* the town. All scenic and peaceful. He forgot the time I spent in other places and that places get under your skin.

Today I'm in here a year – my paper anniversary – half of it spent writing in this book you gave me. One year since I was transferred from the hospital. Anniversaries still stirring up memories. Things we thought were long buried, that for months and months were pushed under the soil in our heads. Well, the land changes. Like an ice age, autumn and winter bring the bones up to the surface. We pick at them, dust them off. Lay them all out on some table like an archaeologist. Take a mental snap of it all. See if those things are how we remembered them.

You can stick anything for a year. People say that when they get a new job and they hate it. 'I'll stick it out for a year.' On my placement, where nobody spoke to me and I felt like the council clown, I never stuck a full year. But I don't mean work, exactly, what I mean is places.

Like two and a half years in Newcastle. It's under my skin. Part of me. Even three days in Edinburgh with Saul and Isaac tripping over themselves to be my mates. Those days were as imperative as any others. I was a different person in a different place. People wanted to know me.

Blake saw me having a laugh with new friends. Then him and his new crew joined up with us. We all got on great. Hunter would always hate me. But when you're being included somewhere you don't care if you are excluded elsewhere.

Those places, even those people, they were the extent of my travels. Three and a half years in Belfast. All those years in the town.

Half years are important. That's why I never leave them out, the things that can happen in half a year: spring to autumn, the flowering, the bursting of the flowers, the dying, leaving everything blank as a canvas, to begin again.

And so I've ended my strike. I'm eating again. Keeping up my strength for all the years and half years I have left here. I'm remembering better for the eating. Thinking stronger. Stopping seeing things that were never there.

29 October

I keep thinking in half years. If they weren't important then a baby could be born six months early and be plump, their organs formed, and they wouldn't be counted as a miscarriage. Like a miscarriage of justice, the word implies that somebody took something – nothing too serious, but blame is definitely inferred.

And what about quarters of years, if I'm so set on fighting the case for half years? No, I won't be pedantic about quarter years, but I still think they matter too. I'll round up for argument's sake.

What about my mum having me three months early? What about me having to stay in special care for months? My granny telling me that it's okay not to visit people in hospital, because some people take it too hard.

'Do you know that when you were a wee baby you were in hospital for a long time? Your daddy never came to see you because it made him too sad, and he didn't know what he could do to help. Your daddy thought that if he looked at you, with all those wires attached to you, that he would cry, and he didn't want to do that, because when a baby hears a person crying they start to cry, and crying takes up a lot of energy that nobody wants to waste. Especially not wee babies who don't have a lot of energy to begin with.'

But, of course, that wasn't why at all.

'Where was Mummy?' I remember asking Granny.

'She never left you, even when I'd get the bus and bring her new clothes, soap and a fresh flannel to wash with, I'd tell her to go and get something to eat but she wouldn't leave you. But that's why you're smaller than the other boys, it's why you have problems when you're playing sports, why you need your puffer, but you won't always, Dr Moore says.'

I'd mind-shelved the months I'd missed until my operation.

Last October, when I woke in hospital, the golden arches were blinking at me through the window. McCruelty. A factory of slaughter and mass production, so the papers say. Good old papers! The yellow was the only thing with any colour. My eyes were drawn. I thought about food. Craved meat. A Big Mac suddenly seemed like a good idea. In for a penny.

I saw my glasses on the table beside me and reached them down, another stab piercing my side. Then I remembered all the craic that came and went before. I fumbled the glasses open and on. It was like my elbows were sown to my sides. I ignored the policeman sitting in the chair, rustling his paper, reaching forward when he saw me wakening and attempting to sit, pressing the buzzer to alert the hospital staff the monster had arisen.

The first officer called for another, who came in from the doorway as if to block it. The newspaper was folded for my benefit: SERIAL GARAGE KILLER CAUGHT, the three-part photo under it, everything dragging itself into focus.

SERIAL GARAGE KILLER CAUGHT? Now, there were many things wrong with that statement. Firstly, it inferred that a garage was killed, which was just ridiculous; secondly, the first time – Bertie Beattie – was Eric's doing. The second time *was* me.

They might have been similar but that wasn't planned. Well, maybe just subliminally. The journalist had no idea that what I'd done was double murder, not serial killing. I just kept thinking: *Serial garage? Serial garage? That doesn't make any sense!* Then I was taken from my thoughts to the hot pain in my side, like someone was sitting on me.

The doctor came in, he nodded at me.

'Mr McAuley, have you just woken?'

'He has,' the officer said.

The doctor looked at him, his mouth puckered like a cat's arse, as if to say, 'He can speak for himself.'

I nodded. I felt sick in the stomach, there was a saline drip attached to my arm. I was just noticing it.

'Scott, you've had an operation. You were stabbed, do you remember?'

'I do, your honour,' I said. I was off my face.

'Is he being funny?' the officer asked.

They are both still faceless to me, their voices warped.

'He's getting his story straight already,' the officer at the door laughed.

'Anaesthetic,' the doctor told him.

He told me I'd lost a lot of blood. Needed a transfusion. I saw him looking at the scars on my arms. I didn't bother hiding them anymore, the fresh cuts and the old ones, done by my own hands and my trusty supply of blades. There, I've said it. They weren't Jasmine's arms, they were mine.

The doctor looked at the officer by the door.

'If you wouldn't mind moving so my student can get in. Is that okay, Mr McAuley, if my student has a look at your wound with me?'

I nodded again.

'Come in please.'

The officer stepped out of the way, and that is when she walked in – although she was fuzzy to begin with, as if she was underwater. Ryley, her hair straightened, nose clean and powdered. She looked twice at me. Maybe it was my head. Shaved, I mean. Yet she must've already known it was me. Things like murder in your pitiful whimper of a town are big news.

She looked dazed, just stared hard while the doctor unstuck the bandage and pulled the few hairs I had on my belly right off.

'It's like getting your legs waxed for us ladies,' Ryley said.

She was no *lady*. She leaned forward and looked at the wound like she was comfortable, but her hands were trembling, her chin gave a twitch. The doctor twisted his neck slowly to scowl at her and she stepped back again, like a naughty child, though she had never heeded authority when she was one.

'You lung was punctured and with your lungs being already underdeveloped, there were a few problems. Yesterday we had to take you back into theatre, but we're certain there will be no more setbacks,' the doctor said, pressing either side of the wound, a single pearl of pus coming out of a gap in the stitches. 'Hmm, you may need an antibiotic. Okay.' He snapped off his gloves, pressed his foot on the bin pedal, the metal clanging around my head.

Ryley never stopped looking at me and I never stopped looking at her. Seven years of looking yet we were different. It was me in the hospital bed and her looking after me, as such. If you could call it that.

I'd gone down that path, same one as her, two kids who people always whispered about. I hadn't made it. How could someone like Ryley, a girl from the ranch who wasn't brought up but dragged up, have ended up all right after her life? Sent to school in her summer dress on snowy days, for one thing. Always clawing the scalp off herself.

She'll probably crack like me someday, do something to balls it all up just months off becoming a legit doc. She'll end up like me, I thought. Not that she deserves to have a bad life, no child does, no matter what life they come from. Look, I can't help this hatred. I don't want it. Never have. I've absorbed it through osmosis.

I really wasn't being spiteful though, I understood Ryley. You know the way there are people you know better than everyone else? There are those who you spend hours of the day with, like classmates and colleagues – those are the people we know. We go home to our families and we all sit in separate rooms, the people we should want to be around, we don't.

Ryley and I were once two runts. Then she was towering over me in my bed. She seemed six-foot tall and was wearing an engagement ring like the Rock of Gibraltar. That made sense. Her mum would never have been able to send her to university unless the latest uncle-dad was Hugh Hefner, but what would Hef want with her? Okay, I'm rambling. The thoughts were hit by the cue ball, heading for every pocket on the table.

What did I know? What *do* I know about anything but the politics of things: the problems, the claims and counterclaims?

Ryley went on in her conversation with the doctor, trying to be Regular Ryley. (Wick name for a doctor. If you ever need surgery, find out if the doctor has a made-up name first! Her mum liked the old Scrabble bag too.) As if she wasn't going to run straight to the phone to say, 'You'll never guess who I was in a room with earlier.'

I remembered her fist twisting like a turtle shell against my back and I remember the 'Teeeacheeer, that wee boy's being cheeky.' Never using my name. Well, I have a name. My name is Scott McAuley. I exist and don't forget it!

'Ryley Richards, my name is Mrs Gillingham,' she'd have said, 'and you are getting too big for this nonsense.' Gillingham would've ignored me though, because I'd have been holding my back, making my chin quiver, and I was too big for that nonsense too. Gurny-Bah was Ryley's name for me.

'Teeeacheeer, that wee boy's nipping me under the table.'

'You were probably annoying the life out of him,' Mrs Gillingham said.

'Do you remember me, *Snotty*?' I asked Ryley. She said nothing, so I nodded at her hand. 'Marrying somebody rich then? Marrying him? The rich doctor?'

Ryley looked mortally offended. She burned her eyes on me, opened her mouth to speak.

'Don't dignify that,' the doctor interrupted, and so she clamped her mouth in that familiar angry line instead. He told me the second surgery had gone well and he'd check in later. 'But sure, you aren't going anywhere, are you Mr McAuley.'

I could've sworn Ryley smirked.

I sat up. The nurses helped to raise me up on pillows. Then I realised how we take our stomach muscles for granted, how buggered we are when they are more of a hindrance than a help. The officer at the window stood so I would know not to try any nonsense, as if I just ran around killing people every day of the week, as if I wasn't feeble and hadn't just been through two operations. Clearly nobody had need to fear me. One nurse set my buzzer out of my reach. 'Can you set that back beside me?' I asked her. She coughed in shock at the nerve of me to ask.

'Sure we'll keep you comfortable,' said the officer closest to the door, giddy at having something decent to do instead of paperwork. Glorified secretary, isn't that what they say? He looked so pleased with himself, dying to get home and tell 'the wife' all about the 'serial garage killer' in the hospital bed. I was being analysed. It was the start of it, officially.

And then Chief Counsellor walked in.

'Sugar Bear!' I said.

He just stood there staring at me as if he was trying to work out if I was real. Really his. And I think I'd proven that we were more alike than either of us wanted. He was silent for so long I ended up saying, 'Why'd you come if you aren't going to speak?'

His eyes were bright from crying. Crying for himself, because he'd never live this down, not on top of everything else. What a Dolly! What a fucking Gurny-Bah!

'I don't know what there is to say,' Duke said.

'Then just go,' I told him.

'The fella, the one you . . . strangled?' He took a deep breath for effect, as if he was being strangled too, by proxy, by talking to me, by sharing my toxic air. 'If it wasn't for him giving that address to his mate before he went there, you'd be dead right now.'

I thought, for a moment, *Duke is relieved I'm alive.* Then Todd came into my mind. Our tussle on the garage floor.

'And Klaudia?' His eyes welled, I'm sure of it.

'Klaudia, is it? First name terms were you?' I asked.

'You little bastard,' Duke whispered.

I shrugged, I looked at the police. Duke could hit me if he wanted, or worse.

'Don't look at them, it's not you they're here to protect,' he said.

He pivoted on the balls of his feet like a loony. *Will I stay or will I go now?*

Yeah, I miss music. I definitely do.

'If you hadn't told Klaudia to lie to me, to pretend to be away, she wouldn't have been caught up in it all. I would never've hurt my sweet honey-skin Klaudia,' I rambled on. The policemen started to look interested while Duke just glowered, that big vein in his forehead bulging at me. 'Aren't you going to advise me to shut up, Sugar Bear? To wait for my solicitor?'

'I don't care what happens to you,' he said, his voice getting big. Defensive.

'Oh, I know that.'

'You are a sick wee boy. And Bertie Beattie. Wha'? A man in his sixties!'

'Bertie? From the village? That Bertie?' I laughed. 'That wasn't me.'

Just the catalyst. Just the turn. Duke sneered at this. No, I wouldn't take the rap for him. Bertie was Eric's. It was only meant to be the one guy. HotToddy. Only meant to be a taste.

'Why? Why that young fella? He was a soldier, a decent person, married . . . a baby on the way.'

Duke was working his way, top to bottom, through his priorities. What you're fighting for comes first. Your children come last.

I laughed.

'I know. That's not on, is it? Married and on dating sites. Todd had to go, you see.'

'You the fucking relationship police now?' Duke shouted. 'Why had he told his mate he was meeting a girl?'

'That all you're worried about?' I asked. 'Well, it wasn't me he thought he was meeting. So you can mourn him now you know he wasn't *a closest gay*.'

'I don't give a shit about gay!' he said.

Like fanny he didn't!

'But two young people . . . that girl,' he said.

Here is a stat Duke can have for the next funeral: more men are the victims of crime. You know that. But the media ignore the fact. They love to make women the victims, so even though two men were dead, and even though Todd and Klaudia both had more miles ahead of them than behind them, no one mentioned him half as much as they mentioned her.

So I went, 'That girl . . . Don't you mean *your* girl?'

And Duke went, 'What are you on about?'

Then I went, 'You were jealous of me and Klaudia. But we were never like that. We were friends but you wouldn't let it be.'

'Don't you start! I phoned your university, you know.'

And I looked at him.

'Oh, aye. It's all coming out now! That dean fella, he elaborated that counselling remark. He *digressed*. Told me, so he did, about that wee girl you were following home from school. Stalking her, you were.'

'Dunno who you're talking about.'

'Mya. Her da went in to see that dean anyway.'

'I didn't do anything to her.'

Not *that* Mya, we were talking about Jasmine now.

'I'd like to hope not. A *twelve*-year-old . . . what were you even playing at?'

'We were friends, okay?'

'Not many fellas would get talking to a twelve-year-old on the Internet then start hassling them to meet up.'

'She's not young. Not that way.' I looked away. 'Jasmine's lived a thousand lives.'

'Who the fuck is Jasmine now?'

I shrugged.

'Could you not've left well alone?'

'Like you left a grieving mother alone? Like you left the married parole officer alone?' Then I said to the officers, 'This is like a soap opera for you two, isn't it?'

'Don't lay any of this at my feet.' Duke paused to add importance to his next bit, which he emphasised like the actor he is. 'Thank God that wee girl had the sense to tell her parents you were *creeping* about.'

Okay, so about what he said, I didn't lie about it. I did say, from the very start, that Jasmine *wasn't* my girlfriend. And the rest, the baby . . . well, I don't know why it's always a daughter I picture. I think it was Mr Banasik writing about Klaudia. Calling her his baby girl.

Everyone seems to be having girls. Todd's *very* pissed-off wife sent me a photo of his newborn, all wrapped in pink. Telling me she'll be raised without a da now. Well, join the club! I suppose it's her version of victim-offender mediation. I'm not doing that again. Not after Mya's mum, the mat-woman.

So that's why *my* baby was born. To give you another dimension of me. God knows I give you very little at the minute.

But I don't know why it was Jasmine I pinned my fantasies on. It wasn't like that. Jas and I used to game together years ago when I was applying to universities. But I had always liked the thought of Newcastle. She was only part of the reason for going.

PrincessJasmine9 she called herself back in the day. Then PJ10, then PJ11. It wasn't until she was PJ12 that they found out about her account. Her photo, her avatar, was just in my head when I was writing. And if she'd have been a suitable age, and the baby was a real baby, Mya was a name I didn't have to reach far for.

I didn't even know her real name until her da showed up at the student house and warned me he'd deal with me himself, no police, if I went near Mya again. All that there. That part was all true. Her da told me that if he thought it'd been going on any longer than it had – it had – that he'd pull the carpet from under me. Called me *boy*. Unmade his point in one syllable.

If I was a kid too, then what was the problem? Sure, even Klaudia said girls mature faster.

No, she wasn't Jasmine at all, but wee Mya; Princess Jasmine taken from her favourite film – Disney's *Aladdin*. She'd put graphics or a filter over so she looked older. When I got there, to Newcastle, and saw that Mya was only a kid I lost all that interest. I thought she sounded young, but you can't always tell.

I waited until she was in secondary school before I introduced myself outside her school. So she was old enough to make up her own mind about me. Listen, I was just acting the big lad when I wrote all that stuff about her.

I just wanted to talk to her. Jasmine. Mya. Whoever she is. I was just taking her temperature at the school gates. She took it the wrong way. They all did.

'Why couldn't you have met a girl your own age?' Duke asked me.

'You had Mum pregnant at seventeen, dead at twenty. So if it wasn't a haemorrhage, if she did overdose, it was because of you. No one kills themselves because of a child.'

He was a smirker too, bad as Ryley.

'Plus you're eighteen years older than Klaudia. But evidently she liked fat old druggies. You're like Jasmine's mum, all off your loser faces.'

'Don't give me that! We both know the truth there, Scott. Mya's ma was decent to you. She's a social worker, for Chrissake. Let you off with your antics. Moving her car out of their driveway and parking it around the corner. Effing with their heads. But when she did that victim-offender stuff with you she didn't know you were a sicko grooming her wee girl. That woman kept your sorry hole out of jail . . . But see what good it does to turn the other cheek!'

Okay. So it wasn't a joyride, or maybe it was, in one of my miniature spurts of rebellion.

'And another thing. They have your drugs, the PSNI,' Duke said.

He looked at the policeman by the window, who was poised, springs in his calves.

'I had a problem with drink in the past but never touched a pill or any of that ould shite in my life,' Duke explained.

'They aren't here for you,' I said. 'It's not the Duke McAuley show anymore.'

'Scott, your mad stories, your fake autograph operation and eBay accounts, your phone, the dodgy pictures . . . who are the photos of? Anyway, it's all being investigated. Just more stuff to bump the years up. And heads up, they don't like your kind in prison.'

The photos were nothing. They were saved from the Internet. Okay, so I did a bit of cropping. They were just something to get Todd where I needed him to be. My part of the bargain.

I said, 'I don't expect anybody to save me. I can do my time.'

'You don't have the strength,' he told me, the leery, laughy Duke McAuley peering through, the Christmas Duke.

'That's right, Duke-boy. You're always right. Always. You stabbed two fellas, younger and smaller than you, but that's one thing. I was the one at the disadvantage with HotToddy.'

'*Hot*, wha'?'

He started towards the door.

I wanted him back, wanted to get him back for Klaudia.

'You know Catholicism is the main religion in Poland, but the passport isn't green, it's red and white. If you blur your eyes you can imagine the blue.'

Duke threw himself on me. Both policemen jumped in and pulled him off. He wrestled against them, then straightened up, rubbed his side. Did himself a mischief. He tucked the ends of his shirt back into his trousers, the funeral trousers. It was a special occasion after all. He was seeing me off for the last time. Breathing hard. A sweat pricking on him from his nanosecond of exertion.

'See? They *are* here to protect me,' I said.

He'd opened my wound again. It was soaking the sheets red. Everybody dismissed the existence of my blood.

'Aren't all nervy now, are you?' Duke said. He walked off then paused at the door. 'You didn't have me fooled for a second.'

'Her hair was in the shower, Klaudia's. In case you think you've got away with *the affair*, you didn't,' I wheezed the words at him.

'Have you got an opening for a new peeler or is it still just taigs you're letting in?' Duke asked the policemen, as if he didn't know. ''Cause there's a great detective there for youse.'

He stared straight through me. 'I never met that Eastern European girl in my life.'

Eastern European? From taig to that! Duke McAuley is what people are talking about when they say 'political correctness gone mad'.

'I saw her once, that Klaudia girl, through her car window, the night she dropped you home last April, after Conor's funeral. I couldn't even tell you what she looked like until now.'

He nodded at her photo. Klaudia was smiling up at us: Bertie, Todd, Klaudia. A trilogy I would watch over and over, even though I missed the first instalment – Bertie and Eric's movie – when it first came out. All I have is Eric's account.

Then it came, Duke's sermon from the book of revelations.

'The lodgers were two girls. Long hair, the both of them. Sure, I was finding their hair in the shower for months.' He spat. 'But you never knew that. Always too tied up in yourself.'

And I knew I'd had the story all wrong. That ombre hairstyle was commonplace after all. Two-toned.

Klaudia. Klaudia. Klaudia.

But answers, when they come, often don't mean a thing. It's

hard to know what's real . . . in here. And it's hard to know what's real in me.

30 October

People never write. They text, they email, they Skype. When you are in prison, and I hope you never are – not this side of the show anyhow, out of the audience and onto the stage – you realise how *little* people actually write.

They send the odd card, the letter telling you that they are let down by you, the offer to look in your eyes, all these strangers wanting to say something to you, the odd bit of fan mail from desperate Staceys who write to you, one hand down their knickers.

But it's the people you are part of, the people you love, which for me means Granny – those people are silent, for the most part. I used to think that there was a tiny chance that I would get out of here and that Granny would still be living.

But I listened to you, even if you think I didn't. I've found myself and lost everyone else in the process.

Anyway, it's enough. I've done this first year in six-month slices. That's the first two done. When they replace my sheets with a new batch, for the next fella, maybe someone will read Granny's birthday card, the Christmas one from Deedee that had a £5 note in it, the letters from Deena and Klaudia's dad, those clippings someone – admittedly not Jasmine, but a sad, lonely Stacey – sent me, which were torn off my wall, shoved down my throat.

Maybe a screw will bin the lot. Perhaps one of the decent ones will give this journal to you like I've requested on the inside jacket.

You'll know that I wasn't bad. Duke McAuley will know that

he was right after all: I'm not strong enough for here, and it's not even spring. I'm contrary like that.

No. It's a fresh October day. Clint will be getting all inspired and the fields on the back roads into town, they'll be like stubble, and the leaves, they'll look like brandy snaps. They've been shedding around the edge of the yard, rustling like a river, escaping their boughs.

Men walk the perimeter. They don't notice these things.

Granny is probably worried about slipping.

Somewhere in the town little kids are lifting the leaves above their heads and letting them rain down on their impressionable, young brains. All of that craic.

Sounds can be heard better this time of year. There is no foliage to catch the noise in, to soften the fall. Bare branches look fraught. The air is chilly and you know it's only going to get colder. This season seems harsh. Everything is being cast away. A blank canvas. A stretch of grey-white sky forecasting the snow that's going to settle on the ground. A quiet grey-white sky perforated by dying branches. A future of hopelessness. The calling off of the search.

But there is promise. You can see a new year from here. If you squint hard enough it's possible. I suppose, for some, there are good things to come, like sun and rain. Like that petrichor.

Tell Duke any of this you want to, if he feels the need to listen, though I doubt he will. Duke knows that the road goes on, he knows how to use his headlights in the dark. But here, tell him, is the end of the road for me.